# EXPONENTIAL

# EXPONENTIAL

## by Adam Cesare

# Dedication

So at this point I've written dedications to
my parents, my friends, and my lovely girlfriend.

Yeah, those people are all of prime importance.
But the folks who buy and read these books? And then the fact
that some of them take the time to write up reviews?

Don't tell anyone, but I think the reader
is the most important part of the equation.

Thank *you*.

# Chapter One

Stealing from the lab hadn't been anything like Samuel Taylor had imagined it would be, and nothing like it would have been if his life were a movie.

There were no sirens or flashing lights. No attack dogs sent to wrestle him to the ground. Although he was fully prepared to, Sam did not have to use the nose of his Ford Taurus to break down the chain-link fence as the guards tried to triangulate his position, and then close in on him with their German Shepherds.

His was not an elaborate heist or an *E.T.* escape. Sam simply exited the Pine Hills facility by waving to the booth guard and driving under the arm of the gate as it was raised above the Taurus, his antenna reverberating like a spring, clipped in his haste. Drive out of the lot was the same as it was every day.

Nobody was the wiser that Sam'd taken anything at all.

It was only one tiny white mouse; even still, Sam knew that he could get in big trouble for taking it.

Three years ago, when he'd first started working at Pine Hills as a custodian, he'd been required to watch two hours of workplace safety films. They were about the handling of hazardous chemicals, proper laboratory procedures and the severity of the confidentiality agreements he'd be signing to work there.

All those videos and he was only going to be a janitor! He wondered how many videos the doctors had had to watch; their orientation had probably taken all day. Two days, maybe.

He'd been working up the courage to rescue one of the mice for the past month, and today, a sunny day in late September, he'd actually done it.

If it hadn't been for the laziness of the scientists that worked in lab 2A, Sam never even would have known about the mice. If his boss wanted to hold anyone responsible, it should be them, because the scientists working in room 2A never fully closed the blinds like they should have. That was how he'd seen the animals.

Sam was in charge of cleaning the hallways, bathrooms and offices of Pine Hill. It was someone else's job to take care of the laboratories, someone who would don a special suit and mask to disinfect the equipment, and someone else's job to take care of the animals. Kind of junior scientists with shorter white jackets. Lab techs. Sam didn't have a degree outside of his GED, but that didn't mean he was stupid, or unobservant. He picked up the lingo here and there, while he ate lunch.

On Mondays, the mice would look normal and healthy, dozing in the corner of their cage, lying on top of each other in a warm mouse pile, or lapping at the water bottle with their little mouse tongues, but as the week progressed they would change.

By Friday, the mice were bloated to twice their normal size, rounded like furry balloons close to bursting. When Sam would come back to work on Monday, the process would start again with new mice, slim and happy and totally oblivious to the fact that by Friday their poor mouse bodies would be bloated and distended. Just thinking of the pain they had to be in, in those final hours, made Sam sad, but he placed his hand over the canvas lunch bag on the passenger seat and felt better.

At least he'd been able to save one.

If someone from Pine Hills were to follow his Taurus back home, they'd see that the theft had been premeditated, and he'd have no way to pass it off as a crime of passion. The week before, Sam had gone to Petco and picked up a small wire cage for his new friend, a miniature version of the water bottle that they used in the lab, bedding, food and an exercise wheel. The wheel was key: he didn't want his new little buddy to put on weight.

Pine Hills was located an hour drive from the suburbs of Phoenix, on a plot of flat, arid, pine-less land to the north. The name might have been someone's idea of a joke if anyone at Pine Hills or its parent companies had ever possessed a sense of humor.

Sam lived an hour northwest of the facility, in a development that was half luxury homes, half affordable apartments. Sam did not live in one of the luxury homes.

He cracked the windows in the car, hoping that the A/C would hurry up and start spitting out cool air. He was sweating into his polo, but it wasn't himself he was concerned with. He needed his new friend to stay cool and comfortable until they got home.

Twenty minutes into the ride, Sam quit checking his rearview mirror at every stop sign. There were no black SUVs or helicopters chasing him. There was nowhere to keep a helicopter at Pine Hills anyway, but somehow in his imagination there were always helicopters pursuing anyone trying to escape from a secret government facility.

All of that was exaggeration, of course. Pine Hills wasn't a secret and it was privately owned, not run by the government. It was *so* little of a secret, that every other week there were protesters outside the gates holding up signs that said "No Frankenfood!" or "The Face of Animal Testing" (those always included a picture of a monkey with its scalp peeled back or a dog with burns all over its body, awful stuff).

Sam couldn't let the mouse free in the car, the little guy would get lost in the seat cushions or squashed under one of the pedals, but he couldn't stand the thought of the mouse suffocating in his lunch bag, unable to breathe with the zipper closed up. Pulling to the shoulder of the road, Sam put the Taurus into park and brought the bag onto his lap.

"I'm opening it, please don't run out and get lost," he said to the mouse. Growing up, Sam had a hamster, a squat wobbly thing that couldn't get anywhere very quickly without treading on its own testicles. Used to the hamster, Sam had a hard time catching one of the mice when he was in room 2A. They were so fast, their white bodies wriggling out from between his big fingers faster than he could close them, afraid the whole time he was going to accidentally hurt one.

Inside the bag, Sam could hear the mouse clawing at the corner, trying to burrow through the unburrowable. The poor thing must have been terrified, locked in there with a quarter of a sandwich and the empty Tupperware that Sam used to pack a dollop of rice pudding for his dessert. Unzipping the bag a few inches, Sam kept his hand over the hole so the mouse couldn't dart out.

"It's okay," he whispered into the hole, angling the light so he could see the mouse. Its pink eyes were wide, its minuscule ribcage rising and falling over tiny lungs, the whole of it covered in soft white fur.

"When we get home you'll calm down," Sam said. "We'll think of a name for you then, too." He didn't know why he was lying to the mouse, it was just a mouse. He'd been thinking of names for the critter all of last week, ever since he'd decided that risking his job for a pet was worth it.

Although frightened, the mouse appeared in good health.

"Hot in there?" Sam asked and pointed the unzipped portion of the bag at the vent. When Sam felt confident that there was enough fresh air for the rest of the trip, he zipped up the bag and continued driving.

"I think we'll call you Felix," Sam said after a while. "It's either that or Ralph, but you look more like a Felix to me."

Sam was having so much fun thinking about their future together that he couldn't hear Felix's frantic clawing at the bottom of the lunch bag.

# Chapter Two

Sometimes the hurt got so big inside of Katelyn that it felt like it was pushing against her eyeballs. The tears relieved the pressure, but never enough to make her comfortable, just enough to keep the bends from killing her.

Fifteen months ago the hurt only visited her occasionally, even when Tommy had been drinking. But since Dale, the hurt filled her every day, only evaporating a bit when she slept, but beginning to fill her up again as soon as she woke.

Tommy used Dale as his excuse to cut out, but the baby had only been that: an excuse. Tommy had wanted to run a long time before the words *crib death* entered their lives. Even the bluntness of the expression couldn't explain the randomness and banality of the syndrome.

They'd done everything right, kept Dale off his stomach. Fed him only formula, scared that Katelyn's breast milk would be unfit for consumption, because of those things she did all those years ago. They even played Mozart for him while he was still in the womb.

None of it prevented Dale from dying.

It had been Kate who found him, his tiny lips blue. And even before she was sure that he was dead, she knew that the hurt would never leave her.

Months ago, when she'd still had a car even though they'd taken the house, she'd driven out of town into the desert, an hour southwest of Vegas, to the bar she used to go to. She hadn't been there in years, but everything about the place was exactly the same. One of the neon signs in the window advertised Zima, and the inside wasn't much more up-to-date. The patrons looked the same too, most of them impossibly wrinkled, bruised and shriveled like old fruit.

The bartender nodded, her appearance not shocking him even though he hadn't seen this particular regular in nearly a decade. Maybe he wasn't surprised because he knew bars like his were magnets, sucking all of their patrons back, even if the pull took a while and had to cross state lines.

She ordered a Bud and waited.

"Haven't seen you around here in a spell," a familiar voice said, its owner lowering himself onto the stool next to her.

Twenty minutes later she was pulled to the side of the road, a glass tube in her lips and the hurt pouring down her cheeks in the form of tears.

This, a short drive south of Vegas, in a bar named Rose's Tavern, was how she reconnected with the love of her life, crystal meth, and the man who sold it to her: Ken Bowman.

Ken sold drugs, but he was nobody's picture of a drug dealer. Tall from birth and slender from his supply, Ken would have looked more comfortable behind the walls of a cubicle at a tech company, his thick glasses, acne scars and Ichabod Crane features more suited to GameStop than the international drug game.

This incongruity extended to his character as well. Ken was warm, kind to Kate in ways he didn't have to be. That night after Rose's Tavern, she'd gone back to his house and didn't leave. There was no sex, not at first, not that night. Ken was just offering her a place to crash and then, eventually, a job.

By the end of that first month, Kate added squatter and drug mule to her CV.

Ken's place wasn't actually Ken's, it wasn't actually anyone's. Their campsites were located in a large housing development with lax security, and with Las Vegas having one of the highest foreclosure rates in the country there was no lack of room if they happened to get chased out of their current squat.

Money wasn't the issue. Ken had a decent car, used it to make deliveries. He just claimed to be a fan of camping. But Kate knew that his reluctance to get a house stemmed more from his meth-fueled paranoia about living "on the grid" than it did his love of butane stoves and sleeping bags.

They'd only been caught once, the security guard who found them chasing them off like they were a pair of harmless high school kids. It was easy to live this way.

Despite the meth, their mock domesticity was a healthier relationship than Kate had had with Tommy. Even their names were a better match: Kate and Ken, like salt and pepper shakers, two parts of a junkie whole.

◆

"Ready?" Ken said, pinching his bedroll at both ends, holding it down with a shaky knee and then cinching a bungee cord around the center.

It was Friday, sometime past noon, and Kate had to be woken up in stages. The only thing that got her moving the third time Ken asked her if she was ready was the anxious itch behind her shoulder blades, the feeling that a day's work would end with a day's pay: a smoke.

"Yeah, I'm ready," Kate said, stretching out until her lower back gave a few muffled popcorn cracks, running her tongue over her teeth. Her front teeth were mossy, but she wouldn't have to worry about them rotting and falling out. The teeth were bridges, extensive, expensive, painful-to-have-installed bridges. Tommy had purchased them for her as a gift, celebrating her first year sober, while she'd been pregnant with Dale.

The dental prosthetics had made her so happy then, but these days they just reminded her of what was underneath: the blackened stubs.

Ken hadn't been so lucky and his smile, even with his limited, occasional use (as occasional as *this thing* could get) had started to dissolve. Yellow lines had formed above his gums, creeping up. Kate had seen enough meth mouth to know what would happen when that yellow waterline reached the top of the enamel: his teeth would begin to recede like a tide, revealing brownish dentin that would make him much less attractive.

Kate tried not to think about it.

"Count 'em, hon," Ken said, tossing her the black Jansport while he poured her a cup of coffee from the thermos. She unzipped the backpack to reveal another bag, clear plastic, filled with dozens of Ziploc sandwich bags, each with ten dimebags inside them. Or at least they were supposed to have ten. That was what she had to find out.

The first time she'd counted, she'd lost track, been so intimidated by the sheer amount of drugs, but now taking inventory of a bigass bag of meth was just part of every Friday morning.

She still only had a loose idea of where it all came from, who Ken picked it up from every Friday before she woke, but it didn't much matter. Pickup wasn't where she earned her keep: she was in the transportation business.

Twenty minutes, sixty-two big bags of ten counted later, they tossed their kit into the back of Ken's station wagon and left. Kate drove, same as every Friday. She was hardly a getaway driver, just better at it than Ken, with steady hands, impeccable parallel parking and three-point turn skills. The two would make the long, windy trip through the suburbs, making regular stops before dipping down 95 until they reached the bottom of the Jansport and their final destination: Rose's Tavern for a hard-earned drink.

They'd never had a problem, never even one detour or routine traffic stop. Today was no different.

Twelve stops, no traffic, and some errant looks from dopeboys and dopemen perched on the edges of windowsills, their bodies half in and half out of the A/C, but nothing too threatening; it was too hot for a stickup. Kate and Ken cut the heat with a nice frosty beer, just one, at Rose's. Then a well-earned Friday night smoke in someone's abandoned living room, Kate trying not to remember the hurt that would surely wake her up in the middle of the night.

# Chapter Three

It was Friday after work and Sam Taylor was pushing the Taurus to its limits trying to get back home. When he'd left for work, Felix hadn't been looking so well. By Wednesday the mouse had stopped running on his wheel and by Thursday night Sam was almost certain that his little buddy was going to die.

It had not been a good day. First he'd mixed wood polish into his mop bucket when he'd meant to pour in Mr. Clean.

A few hours later in the day—unrelated to the Mr. Clean mistake, it turned out—Sam was led into a room and made to talk to some administrator he'd never seen before.

The man had asked him how he liked working at Pine Hills, and then if he'd care to "speculate" as to what "kind of advancements" the lab was working towards. The whole thing was very annoying, with the pencil-pusher taking all of his answers down on a clipboard, and not giving Sam very much time to understand the questions he was being posed, no less think of an answer.

If Sam hadn't been so focused on getting the interview over with so he could clock out and get back to Felix, he probably would have wondered if he was about to get fired.

None of that mattered, though. What mattered was the life of his pet, so today yellow lights meant speed up and red lights were a tepid suggestion.

If this were a cartoon, if Felix had been more Jerry the mouse than flesh and blood, his sickness would have been comical, maybe even a little cute. But this was the real world, so when Felix began to puff up, his skin going springy and the mass underneath soft like a wet sponge to the touch, Sam wanted to cry.

The mouse's extensive weight gain seemed unrelated to his

diet, as he'd had the same untouched bowl of food since Tuesday and hadn't been drinking much water.

This morning, Sam had considered his options, calling in sick to work and taking Felix to a veterinarian, but there was still a tiny amount of fear when he thought about the trouble he'd get in by being found out. And what would the vet be able to do? Sam couldn't tell the doctor what had been done to Felix, even if he wanted to.

Sam parked his car at an angle, not taking the extra second to straighten out the wheel before turning off the engine and taking the stairs two at a time up to his apartment.

Inside, before he even reached the cage, Sam sensed something was wrong.

Over the last week his apartment had smelled different; the slightly rustic tang of wood shavings and mouse turds hadn't been the best scent in the world, but he'd associated it with Felix and thus enjoyed the change. This afternoon his apartment smelled like something else: a messy smell, rusty rainwater, puke and battery acid.

Sam crossed the room, his shoes still on, tracking red Arizona dust from the gravel parking lot onto his living room carpet. He reached Felix's cage, looked down through the wire mesh, and had to stifle a sob.

There was blood on the wood shavings, a surprisingly large amount. Seemingly too much for it all to have been inside one little mouse.

Unhinging the cage door, Sam reached down into the bedding and began to toss handfuls of it aside looking for Felix. Sam had heard somewhere that animals, dogs and cats, would go somewhere secluded and even construct themselves a little nest when they knew that they were going to die, so he figured that must have been what was going on here.

He cringed as his hand brushed fur. It was warm, but not as warm as it should be, with none of the fleshy give that the new, chubby Felix had possessed. Sam pressed his eyes closed and closed his fingers around the shape before lifting it out of the cage. He wouldn't have looked, would have just gone straight to the toilet with Felix's body, a burial at sea, if the fur cupped in his fist didn't feel so…different.

Sam opened his hand, palm up, then peeled open his eyes. It was terrible: Felix had been split down the middle, his body deflated. Now he really did look like a cartoon, but an anatomically correct one: what happens when you *really* drop an anvil on a mouse.

No, that wasn't exactly right. He wasn't squashed, just empty. Where were Felix's bones?

Sam ducked into the kitchen, pulling off a wad of paper towels to wrap over Felix's fur, the Brawny like a burial shroud, before returning to the cage.

There was a slight rustling under the shavings and Sam held his breath, listened. Nothing. It could have been the bedding settling after he'd rustled through it. Or it could be Felix, still alive, but sans fur, the nerves of his body exposed to the air and wood shavings, howling with pain.

Sam picked up one side of the cage, his big fingers leaving brown mouse-blood prints on the plastic, and then tilted the whole thing to the left. The shavings shifted to one side, revealing the green plastic bottom of the cage.

There was nothing there, just some spots where blood or pee had caused the wood chips to clump to the base. He tilted it to the right, the wire exercise wheel rotating slightly on the side of the cage, the food dish spilling pellets.

Tucked against the upper left corner of the plastic was Felix's skeleton.

Not just his bones, but some other parts too: his mouse lungs and heart, still moving. And some other material that Sam did not immediately recognize. He could see them all through Felix's skin, which wasn't skin anymore as much as it was translucent goo.

"Oh no buddy," Sam said, unclear if the oily, sweating cobbling of Felix-parts could hear him or not. Nothing about the mouse moved aside from the gentle steady twitch of his organs, the whole assemblage glued to the side of the cage by Felix's melted non-skin resembling a dense spider web or caked-on lasagna.

It was gross, but the bloodless mass was still his friend, possibly in a lot of pain, so Sam wiped off one hand on a paper towel and reached into the cage to touch Felix, maybe pry him off the side of the cage and cradle him in his hand.

He approached slowly, stopping for a moment as Felix's tiny, eyeless skull shifted in the mass, floating free from the creature's spinal column, the mouse-ball looking like a miniature lava lamp, its contents gently floating inside.

"I'm so sorry they did this to you, Felix," Sam said, not knowing he was crying until a tear splashed down onto his forearm.

He touched Felix's slime, the brownish-snot feeling warmer than he expected, but the mass did not move. It did stick to him, though. He had to give a slight tug when pulling his fingers away, keeping his hand in the cage, but off of Felix's gelatinous flesh.

Assessing his options, Sam thought again of that burial at sea. The mass was warm, but did that mean it was alive? Whatever its state of life, of consciousness, there was no way that his friend was comfortable with his hind legs floating inside his ribcage like that.

Should Sam crush Felix's skull with his, thumb? In order to make sure he was truly at peace before scraping his remains into the toilet?

He never got to answer these or the other myriad questions that swirled in his mind, because there was suddenly a rush of movement as the mass lashed out, its center being pulled towards Sam's hand like metal filings to a magnet.

"Holy shit!" Sam said, frightened, but not pained. His hand was warm where Felix had latched on. The animal's tiny bones poked against the thin flesh at the back of Sam's hand, the tiny butterfly kiss of Felix's beating heart pulsed against Sam's pinky finger, his lungs plastered to his knuckle like a suckerfish.

Sam lifted the whole mess up to his face for a better look and that's when the real pain started.

Felix's teeth, his lower jaw and skull—seemingly independent from each other now—pressed down onto the back of Sam's hand, breaking the skin, the fresh red blood welling up, visible through the goo that held Felix together.

No longer sad for the friend he'd lost, but afraid of the monster that now held tight to his hand, Sam picked up the bloody wad of paper towel and tried to wipe Felix off. The gel only redoubled its grip on Sam, spreading thinner and wrapping itself around his wrist like a fleshy watch. Felix tightened, a snake coiling, constricting as it bit.

The Felix blob continued applying pressure, digging its teeth deeper, touching bone, until it suddenly stopped. Sam quit trying to peel the thing off, looked again at his hand as the goo itself, not the bones, began to tear at the two holes in his skin, expanding the teeth marks and crawling inside his arm, the liquid pulled down into his wounds like pulling the stopper from a drain.

The pain was the worst that Sam had ever experienced, and this was a man who'd once accidentally closed the same hand in a car door, breaking three bones.

"No," Sam said, smacking his hand against the coffee table, trying to smack Felix's heart flat, an attempt to kill whatever gave this thing its power.

The blob didn't like that, redoubling its efforts to burrow inside. Sam saw himself make a fist that he didn't tell his body to make.

There had to be some way to wash it off before it got any further inside of him and Sam thought of the collection of cleaning products he'd stockpiled under his sink, many of which had come from the Pine Hills janitorial supply closet.

Sam didn't make it to the sink, though, dropping to the ground as he tripped over the ottoman that he hadn't wanted in the first place, but the chair had come with it, so what was he going to do? Not take the ottoman?

Sam Taylor died not far from the spot he fell, the tendrils of Felix's new body snaking up inside the flesh and muscle of his arm, around his shoulder, up his neck and finally burrowing into his brain before the man knew what was happening.

# Chapter Four

Vicky Quail held a shotgun shell in one hand and a pair of dice in the other.

It was a good day not to get cooled in a third-string casino. A casino that was *way* off The Strip, so off that it didn't have its own multi-level parking structure, just a bare strip of asphalt lot and a loop out front the main door for taxis.

The shotgun shell wasn't out in the open, of course; even without a gun the ammunition would have seen her kicked out a lot faster than the dice would. No, she had the shell in her pocket for luck, her thumb rubbing back and forth against the head, circling the primer, warming the brass under her fingertip.

"You going?" The old lady next to her pushed in close to speak, got Vicky with a blast of exhalation. Her breath smelled like menthols and dialysis.

Vicky looked at the old lady, shook the dice a few more times just to make sure they were really lucky, not to spite the bat at all, then tossed them.

They hit the back board and rolled to a stop.

*Seven*, motherfuckers.

She knew it without looking down at the felt, could tell she'd won just by reading the pissy expression on the old bag's face and the murmurs around the table. The lady was about to say something, give Vicky another dose of that rancid breath, but then her rheumy eyes flicked up to the shadow.

The shadow got close enough and tall enough that it bumped into Vicky. She could feel the all-too-familiar poke of a clenched fist, the knuckles gliding up her ass and into her lower back. Even without looking, she knew that fist would be concealed by the flaps of an open suit-jacket, the threat meant for Vicky and no one else at the craps table. Having goons visibly threatening guests was bad for business, but some of those guests needed threatening nonetheless.

"Miss. You're not supposed to be here," came a voice from behind Vicky. It was not the guy from last time. Vicky would have recognized the voice.

Even with his knuckles pressing against her, Vicky ignored him and moved some chips off the rack, onto the pass line in favor of the old lady.

Vicky kept her stare across the table, the stickman wringing his hands and giving her a look that said: "Come on, gal, don't make any more trouble for me, I just work here."

Behind her the shadow cleared his throat and Vicky turned towards him, not sure if this bet was going to take anyway, so not *that* concerned with watching the shooter. The Shadow looked pretty much like she'd expected him to: big and flat, all the humor and good nature of a granite slab in a cheap suit.

The Shadow didn't move backwards, he didn't give her tits an inch of room, his knuckles now against the baby fat of her belly. This man was a professional.

"Oh come on, dude," she said, trying to sound SoCal but coming off hill-person, the accent she would forever have, no matter how hard she tried to shake it. "It's not like I'm counting cards. I was barred three years ago, haven't I earned back? Were you even around back then?"

"Life is life," he said, practicing his tough-guy-ese, clearly. She imagined him driving to work, flipping over books on tape from side A to side B and repeating after the narrator.

"So I'm magically counting dice? If that's the case then why have I been down for the past hour? Am I counting sides? Here's a hot tip for ya: there's six."

The fist loosened, just for a moment, becoming a hand that wrapped itself around her wrist, pulling Vicky's hand out of her sweatshirt pocket.

"You think I'm cheating? What kind of amateur do you take me for?" she said, keeping her hand balled around the shell, really regretting her choice of good luck totem for the day.

He gave her wrist a slight shake, whipped his eyes down to look at the shell, and then curled her fingers back up for her, covering it.

"Planning a stickup or just a killing spree?" he whispered, bending his body down to Vicky's level, no easy feat for the big man. Next to them, the old lady was unable or unwilling to hear him so there would be no rescue from her.

"Okay, you got me. I guess I'll be going," Vicky said, trying to keep the tremor out of her voice. Somehow a night in a cell or a boot in the ribs was feeling way possible now, popping the cherry-flavored optimism cloud she tried to keep afloat of at all times.

"I think you should come with me and have a conversation. Take your chips," he said, nodding to the stickman, watching the small stack come back across the line, doubled because the old lady had won. The casino was putting on a show to seem amicable, at least, but she doubted she'd be allowed to keep that money.

"Ya know what, I don't feel comfortable taking these, since you think they're ill-gotten," she said, selecting two stacks of four from her rack, laying them flat against the railing and motioning to the stickman and dealer, leaving him a toke.

Gathering up the rest with her free hand, she pressed the chips into The Shadow's shirt, rubbing them up against the flaps of his suit jacket and opening her hand so they sprinkled all over the floor.

"I am *so* sorry, could you help me with those?" she said, and then louder, in case the surveillance system had sound *and* video: "I think one or two might have slipped into your pocket."

The Shadow let go of her wrist, clearly not a fan of this trick. He raised his arms and flicked his eyes up to one of the black lumps protruding from the ceiling, looking at his pit boss through the camera, his expression a question.

Vicky didn't wait to hear the answer. She ducked around him and walk-ran to the nearest exit, hands down at her sides, but pumping.

Hitting the parking lot, she sprinted to her van and jumped inside. She was two grand poorer and her bankroll felt the hurt.

A couple miles away, when she was sure she wasn't being followed by men who preferred to use their clubs for full-contact golf, she pulled into a Carl's Jr. to take stock.

She'd lost all the chips, but kept her hand around the shell, the brass still hot and sweaty as she pulled it out of her pocket and looked at it.

It could fit in either of the shotguns pegged to the carpeted walls behind her, but not in the two rifles under those. Those took 243 cartridges, silly.

Only one of the guns had been her father's: a break-action shotgun that was basically an antique, the kind of weapon that made you confident in your skills when you hit (it only held two shells) and suffer an acute sense of self-loathing when you missed. It barely got any use, but she kept it clean, fired it every once in a while just for the nostalgia factor.

Below the gun rack she had enough ammunition and Sterno that at least she'd never go hungry, provided she could afford enough gas to get her out far enough into the wilderness to hunt.

Vicky opened the glove box, counted out enough change to hunt up a burger, and then hit the drive-through as she considered where she should head next.

# Chapter Five

It wasn't the sunrise that had woken Harold Graham, but pangs from his lower intestine. Although, as he opened his eyes, the sunrise was there too and the car around him was a cold blur.

Reaching blindly to the dashboard, he found his glasses, replaced them on the bridge of his nose, wiped a glob of spittle off the clipboard in his lap and looked up at the apartment.

There was no movement, no lights.

He directed his gaze to the next row of cars in the parking lot. Taylor's Ford Taurus was still there, still parked at the same odd angle, unmoved. Unless that was how the guy always parked it, which wouldn't have much surprised Harold. Something about Sam Taylor had seemed askew, maybe a little Peter Pan-y, definitely a little slow.

Harold knew that the man was keeping a secret before he'd asked his first question, before either of them had sat down. It was in Sam Taylor's fidgeting and his moist handshake. To Taylor's credit, he hadn't caved, hadn't confessed to any wrongdoing when Harold had asked him if he'd ever been inside lab room 2A.

"No sir, that's not my job. I clean the hallways, lavatories and staff-spaces," Sam Taylor said, repeating the same thing more than once. It had sounded rehearsed, but at least the guy had been rehearsing the right lines. Name, rank and serial number: he knew to give Harold nothing more and nothing less.

Harold wasn't going to get him to produce the animal without a fuss.

That was why he'd woken up freezing, having fallen asleep in the company car. The night before he hadn't been able to race Taylor home from work and had spent the evening waiting for Taylor to leave, to run an errand or something. Apparently that had been a mistake.

The janitor hadn't even called out for pizza, probably had a stack of Red Barons queued up for all of his quiet nights in.

Corporate Investigator wasn't as cool a job as it was a title. There was no secret-agent stuff, no high-level espionage, only stern questions regarding the occasional off-color joke told around the bubbler or errant cupped breast at the company Christmas party. Harold was the grown-up equivalent of a high school assistant principal.

This, sleeping in his car for a stakeout, was the most excitement Harold had ever seen on the job.

There was no use waiting for Taylor to vacate his apartment, as there was no guarantee that he would be leaving today at all, not without work.

"Fuck this," Harold said to the empty car, his stomach grumbling. He was more than ready to take his morning shit but had no bathroom.

The air outside the car had already begun to warm, the sun barely up, the frost in his breath getting lighter by the second. It would be another hot day, to add to the pile of hot days, the normative mode of his homeland. The members of his family were all so pasty, so burnable, why the hell had they never left Arizona?

There were stairs leading up to Taylor's apartment. Harold hated stairs and thus Harold hated Sam Taylor by extension.

Chilly or not, there was sweat dripping down the crown of his head, over his forehead and down his nose, slicking the bridge of his glasses as he climbed.

On top of the sweat, his pants were about to be filled. If Taylor didn't answer on the first few knocks, he was going to have to squat behind the fence, where he couldn't be seen from the road. All that coffee had seemed like a great idea to stay alert for the stakeout, but he really should have thought the rest of it through. Harold had an irritable stomach and without time to prepare, he hadn't thought to bring a cup of his probiotic yogurt for breakfast.

Harold knocked on the door to Taylor's apartment, and then flicked on his phone while he waited. It was five minutes after six. There were very few people who got up this early on a Sunday. He hoped that Taylor, that Forrest Gump motherfucker, was one of them.

A pocket of gas worked itself loose and slid out of Harold. There was no relief to the fart, though, only the feeling that he was running out of room in his bowels and that evacuation was imminent.

Harold knocked again, harder and using the side of his fist, not the knuckles.

"Mr. Taylor?" he asked.

There was movement somewhere behind the door, possibly Taylor tripping over his own pants, too dumb to dress himself.

"Mr. Taylor, it's Harold Graham, from Pine Hills," he said. There was a mouth-sound behind the door. It could have been a yawn or a groan. "Mr. Taylor, could you please hurry up? I need to use your bathroom."

He hadn't planned on saying that, it had just happened. This guy was dicking him around: mouth-breathing on the other side of the door, probably trying to stash evidence. Evidence that, frankly, Harold really didn't give a shit about at this point, he just needed to take a crap.

Now the sound was more of a gasping, a choking, something dragging along the space right behind the door.

A scenario worked itself around in Harold's mind. The story was not the result of Holmesian deduction, but instead a wildly improbable *Unsolved Mysteries* reenactment.

In his mind's eye, Harold saw Taylor sprawled out behind the door, a spilt bowl of cereal on the carpet in front of him. What kind of cereal? Something big enough to choke on, yet childish enough that Sam Taylor would buy it, let's say Cookie Crisp. The shock from Harold's arrival had caused the guilty party (Sam Taylor) to gasp, inhaling a mouthful of Cookie Crisp and blocking his airway. Right now Taylor was clawing at his throat for air, compacted lumps of milk and corn syrup blocking his airway.

"Mr. Taylor are you okay?" Harold screamed through the door, the sweat rolling down his balding head in torrents now, a flood about to wash his glasses right off his face.

There was more movement, more gasping, then an odd sound, something he'd never heard come out of a person, not in a CPR training video, not anywhere.

Harold tried the door, even though he knew these units must have automatic locks. The knob wouldn't move.

"I am kicking in the door, Mr. Taylor. Move away if you can. Hang on!" The pain from his intestinal distress melted away in a haze of adrenaline and real-police work, or what he imagined real-police work would feel like.

As Harold braced himself on the railing behind him, he

looked down over the ledge and got a flash of vertigo from the second-floor height. If he couldn't break it down in one go, he'd have to try not to bounce off the door and flip onto the walkway below.

Pushing away from the railing, he brought his right foot up and kicked, his shoe connecting just above the lock. The door didn't budge and instead Harold felt a tear at his thigh that he *prayed* was his pant leg, not a ligament or muscle twanging loose. For a brief moment after impact, the blow turned his leg into a tuning fork, the length of it vibrating with pain.

He bit back a scream as he hopped away from the still-intact door, not wanting to give himself too much space to dwell on whatever damage he'd just done.

*No time, use your shoulder,* he thought and then quickly hoped that one of Taylor's neighbors was an early bird, ready to come help him get in, should his second attempt fail too.

There was no proof that Taylor was really in trouble, no indication that he wasn't hearing the TV or something, but in his addled state, just waking up, having to shit, Harold just wanted to break something down.

Holding his arm, trying to angle the shoulder padding of his sports coat down to fully cover the bone, Harold rocked himself into the doorway.

It did not spring open, but it did crack, the corners of the door splintering in its frame. These new apartments were built like hotels, built to withstand drunken frat parties and break-in attempts, not to protect the tenants, but the landlords. Even though the door wasn't yet down and his leg was humming, Harold took a quiet kind of pride in getting the door this far with two knocks.

Only one more knock and it would be open.

Harold sucked in a breath, rubbed his shoulder and tried not to imagine the bruise he'd have tomorrow. Should he switch to the other shoulder? Try to spread the damage out instead of taking it all on one side?

This was the line of reasoning he'd been entrenched in when the door, already partially broken in, exploded outwards, pushed from the other side until the frame and hinges splintered towards him, the door pushing him off of the second-floor landing like a prize in an arcade's bulldozer machine.

There was a brief—fantastically brief—moment where Harold

Graham pondered what the hell could have pushed the door towards him with such force. That moment was about fifteen feet long. The only pondering he did after that was how many bones he had broken, and if he was going to die, splattered on the concrete walkway.

The answer, was no. He would die long before enough blood could seep out of the multiple compound fractures he'd sustained during both the initial collision against the door and then the fall to the concrete.

With the one nostril that was not streaming blood, Harold could smell something awful and for a moment was embarrassed that he'd have to be loaded into the back of the ambulance with shit dripping down the legs of his khakis. But then he heard movement from the second floor and the beast jumped down, landing in front of him with a soft splat, sixty pounds of fetid meatloaf and gravy hitting concrete.

The smell wasn't coming from Harold.

The beast, about the size of a mid-range dog, broke none of its own bones on the way down from the landing. At about five feet away, Harold was able to get a good look at it before it moved towards him.

A good look and far too good a smell.

The creature's membranous body moved with the gentle fluidity of a snail, with the bones underneath giving it weight, heft and locomotion. The bones, fully visible from the outside of its body and human in appearance, were bare except for flecks of muscle. There were organs too, but they looked foreign, nearly primordial, big amoebas fluttering and floating with pronged flagellum. The guts and bones and translucent skin cobbled together to give the beast nothing approaching the structure of a human or animal that Harold had ever seen.

At the nightmare's base, there was a human ribcage. It was bifurcated, the tips of each rib undulating like the long legs of a house centipede, inching the monster forward across the concrete. Behind that was a collection of femurs and finer bones (forearms maybe?) reconfigured into two large cricket legs, bowed and ready to spring.

Harold lifted his hands to protect himself and noticed for the first time that one of his fingers was broken at an angle, the nail facing the wrong way.

He whimpered at the sight of the busted pointer finger and the beast reacted to the sound. The creature pushed itself flatter against the walkway, most of its loose bones shifting away from Harold, not frightened, but the body language of an animal that was ready to pounce.

There, floating along with the bones, stuck to the creature's side like you might collect a piece of toilet paper on your shoe, was the eyeless face of Sam Taylor.

"Someone please help!" Harold was able to shout before the beast was upon him.

It did not crush him with the power of its bones, not at first, but instead used its gooey flesh to push into Harold's wounds.

It didn't seem too concerned that all of itself wasn't going to fit inside of Harold's body. The creature was not some covert alien invader looking to replicate Harold's every movement, learn his ways.

No, the creature was after his liquids and solids. It crawled inside Harold, the pain excruciating as it snaked into his legs and arms, but then so much worse as its mass reached his internal organs, pressing his bowels empty, filling his lungs and then moving north.

It took almost a full minute, but eventually the incursion was enough to dislocate Harold's head from the rest of his body, putting an end to both his tenure as the Pine Hills Corporate Investigator and his life.

# Chapter Six

David Nez awoke to gunfire, wiped the sweat from his chin and checked the clock. It was very early.

Like most mornings, he would wait and determine whether the gunshots were internal or external, whether they were on the streets of the suburbs or products of his subconscious.

It was a rarity, but this morning they were real. Out in the night there were two more pops in close succession. Nez groaned and began getting dressed.

It was only when he'd done up the last button on his shirt that he realized that, yeah, this wasn't his job anymore.

He'd never been a regular sleepwalker, but when he was a kid there was a time he'd put on jeans and a baseball cap and stepped into a cold shower before waking up. This was like that, the gunshots triggering some kind of police instinct inside him, convincing his half-sleeping brain that it was time to get up and go to it.

But Nez wasn't a cop any longer. He wasn't even in New Mexico anymore. Far from it. He still had his uniform, though. The same one he'd been wearing when he'd bought a car, turned in his gun and badge and left the Navajo Nation Police.

You were only supposed to hand in the gun and badge, right? You got to keep the rest? He was unclear on the procedure.

People getting shot in Henderson—or did the echo of the shots travel across that invisible line, float in from Vegas?—weren't his problem.

But now that he was up, there would be no getting back down. It was the same most nights, awoken by a sound, a gunshot that may or may not have been a gunshot, and then up for the rest of the night. Even if he were back in Crownpoint he wouldn't have gone back to sleep. If someone had already radioed in and caught the shots before he could, it would have been time to spend the remainder of the night on some paperwork, maybe drive around town.

Even after the force, Nez did paperwork in Henderson, too, but it was just pretend police work.

To keep his mind occupied, Nez would use the internet to read up on crimes in the area, puzzling over them like you might the crossword, if you had a better vocabulary and were less into blood-spatter patterns than Nez was.

Nez moved from the foot of the bed to his small desk and took the computer out of sleep mode. He never turned it all the way off when he was getting in bed. Why bother?

The clock on his nightstand told him it was a quarter to three, but that clock was off by about ten minutes. Not that it mattered at this time of night.

Clicking open a few new tabs in his browser, he started local and moved national. One of the CNN headlines stopped him.

*Mutilated Remains Found in AZ Development*

The item was local-ish, depending on where it was in Arizona. Besides, how could Nez resist a headline like that?

There wasn't much to the article, though. No pictures of the body aside from a bloody white sheet spread over concrete. The mess had been discovered yesterday morning by an unnamed caretaker while out on his rounds. Police were unsure if the attacker was animal or human, but the caretaker had voted for animal and claimed to have scared whatever it was off when he pulled up in his souped-up golf cart.

"It was weird looking. Just ran behind the complex and into the wilderness when I honked." What a poetic quote. The reporter had probably gotten wood, taking that one down. The caretaker was willing to talk, the police less so. All they said was that they were looking into the crime and related apparent home invasion (whatever that meant, the article didn't elaborate).

That the police were less than forthcoming didn't surprise Nez.

In the weeks and months after he'd quit the force, he'd tried out security jobs like the one that guy had. The shifts ended after eight in the morning and there's usually not much to do between midnight and quitting time but drink, chew breath mints after you got paranoid you were going to be caught drinking, and try to get up enough speed in your golf cart to peel out.

If the rent-a-cops were blowing a point-one-three by the time the cops took his statement, like Nez bet he was, they weren't going to lean too heavy on anything he said.

Interesting, semi-local, but no real police work to be done on Nez's part.

He clicked onward, skimming through headlines about politics and looking for crooks that *could* be caught, would hopefully be caught.

After reading through a few more articles (an old woman covering up the accidental death of her husband and catching heat for it, some punks playing a game called "Sock the Jew" which had resulted in a fractured skull for some poor fucker, a handful of anonymous, but no-less-depressing random acts of violence), Nez was tired of armchair, imaginary police work and decided to go for a drive.

This, too, was part of his nightly ritual. He liked to kid himself that he was "choosing" to take a cruise, but it was the illusion of choice: David Nez needed to drive his truck.

Nez's truck was a 1991 F150, the kind that came with a paint job that wasn't sure if it wanted to toss out the eighties entirely so it kept that lengthwise double-stripe along the side. He climbed in, using the driver's side headrest as a handhold with some of the petrified cushioning crumbling out of a tear in the upholstery. A few years ago, he would have been concerned with the deterioration and started trolling the internet for a replacement headrest, but now he didn't care. Besides, his new job didn't pay enough to go blowing his money on nonessentials.

Even security jobs, with the equipment limited to a keychain of pepper spray, a prepaid cell and a Maglite, had proven to be too much stress for him. Sitting guard saw him working up acid in his esophagus, if he let the stillness spook him and started thinking about what would happen if he had to do something real and lay down his life for whatever warehouse he was guarding.

So he'd given up on that and found the most well-lit, low-stress job he was able to with his limited work experience and training: telemarketing.

He used to think those people were the devil. Turns out, they were just sad and underpaid. Like he was now.

Turning over the engine, Nez checked his watch. It was about five hours until he had to be back at the call center, which meant that he could travel approximately two hours away from his current location, burning up about half a day's pay worth of gas in the process.

The trip would be worth it, he told himself as he rolled the truck through deserted Henderson suburbs, dipping down to the more populous outskirts of town. Or at least more populous at this time of night, if not the daytime.

In the shaded windows of the love motels there were lights. Along the top row of doors, one or two were open a crack, unengaged ladies inviting johns in for a late night party. Below the landing, in the parking lots, cars rocked gently, their drivers too cheap, too drunk or in too much of a hurry to rent a room. Nez couldn't tell if that tug in his soul was because he wanted to go knocking on windows, make some busts, or whether he yearned for the touch of another human being. He sped up to pass the motels, terrified to find out.

After the liquor stores thinned (Nez keeping his speed up to get by *that* tug, too) there was nothing but road. This was why Nez woke, he told himself, the hills and the desert and the scrub, all discolored by his headlights, whipping past like it could go on forever. Which it wouldn't, of course, eventually he'd reach Rose's and his nightly sojourn would be halfway done, the return trip feeling less special because he'd already seen that same emptiness once already tonight.

He'd never been inside Rose's Tavern.

Most nights the bar was closed by the time he arrived in the parking lot, but he would always stop and watch, take in whatever activity there was to see. Sometimes it was drunks necking on the way to their cars, if he was early, but most nights there was no one.

Even if he was just watching the critters duck in and out of the brush surrounding Rose's Tavern, Nez enjoyed himself. He thrilled at the occasional owl hunt, rooting for the owl just a little bit, even though he liked the mice and snakes too, felt for them.

Tonight the lines of the road seemed about as close together as they ever got. Nez was an insomniac, but that didn't mean he wasn't tired. As he drove through the nothingness, passing the occasional trucker, he knew that he was tempting fate. It was quite likely that one day he'd fall asleep pushing eighty and end up adding his own rock formation to the scenery.

Rose's kept the lights on all night, even after they'd locked the doors for that magic three-to-nine rest period, and Nez could see the familiar blue glow of the bar's chicken-wired windows up ahead.

Choosing Rose's as the place he stopped his laps had been arbitrary. There were other businesses in the area, not close, but within a few miles. A diner would have been a smarter choice to stop at. At least he'd be able to get a cup of coffee for the ride back, but the tavern was his spot.

Nez pulled off the road onto the dirt parking lot a bit too fast. He had been tired, near loopy, but the crunch of gravel woke him and he enjoyed watching the dust settle.

He checked his watch again as the engine cooled. He'd made good time, enough for a sort of siesta, if he allowed himself.

Nez listened to the nothingness. The large air conditioner angling out of one of the tavern's windows would sometimes hum for a short moment, completing a money-saver cycle. Money saver or not, the owner must have forgotten to turn it off and was costing himself (herself?) electricity to turn the bar into an icebox in the desert night.

David Nez fell asleep while running through telemarketing scripts in his head. He thought of the samey conversations he would begin to have in a couple of hours, and was comforted by the fact that there was no way he would be awoken by a gunshot out here, under the stars, with no goddamn people around.

# Chapter Seven

In Jake Bartlett's estimation, there were only two ways to use a day off from school:

The early way and the late way.

They weren't just settings on a clock, times of day, they were philosophies, Taos.

Jake was a sophomore now, rising in three months, so he'd had time as a teenager to dabble in both methods, but he preferred the early approach.

Many of his friends would opt for the late route, rolling out of bed around noon, flipping on their Xboxes and spending the rest of the day fragging whilst finding new and inventive ways to integrate racial and sexual slurs into their conversations. Some of his friends had central air, some of them didn't, but at that point in the day, it would be too hot outside for them to do much of anything else.

Not that Jake didn't enjoy that kind of thing—video games and swearing—but he'd been turned on to the joys of the early path a few years ago and would now set an alarm on any day off, a full hour before he would normally have to wake for school.

He'd chanced upon this ritual on a Memorial Day back in middle school. His mood towards mornings had not been markedly changed when he'd first woken before his parents, walked his mountain bike out the garage door. But he was amazed how cool the pre-dawn air was, how it held a crispness the likes of which he had never felt outside of Christmas time.

From that first morning, he was hooked by the freedom that rides in the forest offered him, and even though he'd gone out many times since, each time he always found himself chasing that initial rush, never attaining it.

Back then his bike had been an off-the-rack Mongoose that had taken six months for Jake to "grow into" and comfortably pedal (he was a late bloomer), but that didn't stop him from spending Memorial Day blazing trails in the hills behind his family's house, blisters on his heels.

Even if he'd never again feel that high, the trips allowed him to maximize his time free from the shackles of school. These times untethered him from society, allowed him to revel in a full day without rules and schedules.

Most of his friends lived either on his street, Indian Hill Road, or one block over on Oakmont. During the period where they were old enough to be allowed out of the house by themselves, but before they became "mature" enough that they only viewed the woods as a place to drink and smoke, his friends would join Jake in tear ass-ing around Prescott National Park on their mountain bikes, then later on their dirtbikes and ATVs.

This morning, Jake left his room and walked down the hall, not turning on any lights as he made his way through the house. The darkened family room was a mess, but he moved with a kind of pre-ternatural awareness of the stacks of laundry and clutter that impeded his progress. In the kitchen, he filled his canteen and hitched the strap around his waist before pushing through the door to the garage.

Even though he was up with the dawn this morning, the air was not as cool as that first day, four years ago. Still he could feel his skin pucker as he lifted up the garage door, trying to take most of the weight on his legs, but leading more with his back.

The garage door had a motor, with a switch right beside the entrance to the house, but running the chain was noisy and he didn't want to wake his parents. Not any earlier than was absolutely unavoidable. The ATV was a beast and when he turned over the ignition, there would be no avoiding waking his parents, possibly even the Clarks in the next house over.

His neighbors were nice enough people, but Jake didn't have any sympathy for their son Tod. If that too-cool bastard wanted to sleep in, bemoan Jake's attachment to "hanging out in the woods and doing baby shit", then fuck 'em.

Jake took his keys from his front pocket, inserted the smallest of them into the ignition, twisted his hand around the accelerator, dropped his toe to the starter and let the quad roar under him.

A couple years older than he was, the all terrain vehicle was a 1993 Suzuki Quadsport 230, its body a battered white plastic and its cushions even worse, a dark purple that had been bleached bright by the sun. Jake and his father had purchased it used, but while his parents were willing to scrimp on the bike itself, Jake's helmet was brand new, top of the line with a small brace to protect his neck. The helmet was too large to be cool, with a mouth vent that whistled while he breathed, but Jake was still happy he had it, should he ever find the twenty-one-year-old Suzuki lying on top of him. Besides, there was nobody around to see him or his blocky helmet.

Even with daylight savings and the dawn coming earlier these days, the sky was still mostly dark at a quarter after five.

Jake decided to take the long way out of the garage, driving out onto the street instead of through the backyard and straight into the forest trails that bordered his house.

The engine sounded like a giant hornet, its clatter unpredictable as it warmed, an arrhythmic hum that did not correspond to his wrist on the acceleration.

With their sharp peaks and trembling valleys, the vibrations made it feel as if the bike could explode under Jake at any moment, but he was confident that it wouldn't.

Reaching the end of the driveway Jake peeled out on the asphalt, performing a tight mini-donut that added another brushstroke of black rubber to the design he'd been working on since the last time the city road crew had been through and replaced the tar. The turn brought him around, pointed him in the right direction so that he could zip up past the house, hit the start of the trail in an explosion of dirt and pine needles as his tires acclimated to the change from lawn to forest floor.

In most of its hilly areas, Prescott didn't have dense woods, which meant that making excursions from the bike paths was not only doable, but something Jake Bartlett tried to attempt every time he went out on an early morning ride. These days off were special occasions, after all.

These explorations of the unknown made him feel like he was properly utilizing his time off, even if he was still only tooling around in the same few mile area, the same square of the map. Jake had ten years of scout training, GPS on his phone, and decent reception, so there was never any real danger that he'd go missing.

Taking the ATV off the packed dirt of the path, he could feel fallen branches pulverized under his tires. Flecks of mulch dusted the hairs of his legs, branches clattered against his facemask, leaving green streaks, and the occasional splinter got too far up his shorts that he'd have to stop and remove it, lest he pierce his ass when he crashed back down onto the seat.

Ascending to a hilltop, entering unfamiliar territory, Jake slowed as he approached the ridge. He was young and reckless, but he wasn't suicidal. He knew that jumping his ATV off an unknown incline could find him plummeting off of a sheer drop, landing into the mass of a fallen tree, the branches impaling both his bike and his body.

He stopped at the crest, the Quadsport idling under him, the wheeze of the engine still loud enough to scare away any wildlife down in the valley below him.

The incline of the hill wasn't steep. He would have been able to cruise right over it, but he was glad he'd stopped: the view was magnificent.

Instead of removing his helmet, he raised his visor so he could look out at the world without its slight tint.

The sun was just over the canopy now, its rays visible as the humidity of the morning burned off, bars of light shooting out in cartoon lines that skimmed across the treetops, deflected by the pale blue-green of fir needles. The stars of the cosmos were still visible as Jake inclined his head far enough to see behind where he was sitting.

With the only sound the idling engine and his own breathing in his helmet, it felt as if he were in space.

Taking in all this beauty, enjoying nature without a whiff of irony, would get Jake called a fag if any of his friends had accompanied him.

This was the wild. And it was his. *What he jerked off to had no bearing on that ownership.*

As he looked into the distance and ruminated on this, both disturbed by the frankness of his feelings and awestruck by the view, it took a moment longer than it should have for him to register the movement down in the clearing below.

There was a bear, rubbing its body up against one of the clearing's few trees. Seemingly unperturbed by the sound of Jake's engine, the large bear pressed its back against the tree and proceeded to scratch, not really scratching at all but instead putting its scent on the trunk.

It was a black bear, not a rare sight in this area if you were hiking, but not something you saw often if you stuck to the suburbs, at least not if you had your trashcans sealed tight. The bear was too large to be a juvenile, and its behavior combined with the fact that he was a big mother, meant it couldn't be anything but a full grown male.

Standing on the ridge with the path visible behind him and the bear and clearing down below him—the divide between the mundane world and the wild made literal—Jake Bartlett began to compose a list of facts:

It may have been large, but a black bear was not a grizzly.

It was over a football field away, at least, and it would have to run uphill to get to him.

It wasn't an off season for a sighting so the bear would probably not be aggressive, either from hunger or because it was in the process of snapping out of its hibernation period.

It was rubbing itself vigorously, almost playfully: this was a bear in a good mood.

Jake considered this list, and with a nagging sense that his action was less a taking in of calculated risk and more an expression of his rarified rebel soul, Jake reached over the handlebars, grabbed the key and switched off the engine.

*There. That was it.*

It hadn't been the cool air that had caused his senses to snap into focus that Memorial Day, it was the sense of adventure, it was the potential the forest had held, the idea that he was going out into it alone, friends, parents and society be damned.

Back then the sense of adventure had been linked to the goose bumps of an unseasonably cool morning.

Now it was rising up from the stillness of the forest, quiet enough that between breaths he could hear a distant woodpecker, the rustle of the bear's fur against the bark.

Before he could ask himself what he was doing, how close he was willing to get, Jake was already taking a second step down the hill, his foot sliding out from under him on a sheet of dry brown pine needles.

If the bear heard him slip and fall gently onto his ass, it didn't show it. The animal just kept rubbing, getting the side of its head in on the action now, the forest quiet enough that Jake could hear its panting.

*Maybe he's not playing, maybe he is in pain.*

The thought stopped Jake, caused him to look away from the bear and the tree for a moment and then look back at the situation with fresh eyes, the way some optical illusions could only work when you weren't looking for them.

Upon further appraisal, fifteen yards closer now after a few more steps, it was clear that the bear was favoring its left side, the fat of its haunches jiggling as it threw itself against the tree.

Jake thought of several fail videos he'd seen, fat girls attempting to twerk, hurting themselves in the process, and he giggled.
The bear heard that, a teenage nerd's cruel laughter, and looked up at Jake.

Even from the distance of a short city block, the animal was able to pinpoint Jake's gaze immediately. Jake tried to stand still but found it difficult to find balance, his weight shifting on the exposed roots under his sneakers. The noise caused the bear to vocalize, the sound not quite a roar but more than a whine.

Ranger Rick time was over. Without turning his back to the animal, Jake would need to walk up the ridge and get on his Suzuki. They were more likely to charge if you fled.

The sensitive boy, the stereotypical late-bloomer he was, made it hard for Jake to look at an animal and not anthropomorphize it.

Especially one with big, expressive, dog-like eyes, two golden tufts on his black face, right where the eyebrows would be on a human. Standing tall, its eyes were telling Jake that the bear was confused, in pain, that it wanted Jake to help.

And maybe, if Jake wasn't willing to help, the bear would be satisfied with cracking his ribcage open, sucking out his organs and bone marrow.

Lowering itself to all fours, the bear began to pad forward, diving to the ground and rubbing its back and side in the dirt.

Jake raised his left foot slowly and placed it behind him. It may have been a coincidence, but the bear took two steps to counter.

He could see its back now. Dirt, twigs and pine needles clung to the bear's fur. Well, not clung, but were stuck there, spackled by a layer of something that glistened in the rising sun. While the bear was busy marking the tree, the tree had been busy covering the bear with its sap.

Red sap.

Blood.

A few scenarios filled Jake's head, ranging from sad to terrifying. There was one with hunters—poachers, really—scoring a glancing blow and then losing track of their prey. Then a vividly familiar one where the bear got a tiny bite from a bat with rabies, its brain beginning to melt so that it was forced to rub itself bloody on the tree.

The bear was bounding towards the edge of the clearing now, would be scaling the hill towards Jake in seconds. He could hear its breath, ragged, frothing with exertion. How could Jake have seen the bear for anything else but what it was: mad with pain? Did he need glasses?

Jake's rational mind knew that it was time to make a decision: Did he turn and run to the bike, losing sight of the bear and possibly antagonizing it further, or did he keep his steady backwards march, confident that he would be able to start the ATV in one kick and be gone?

That's when the blood caked onto the bear's back started to move.

Not pump, not flow, not spurt.

No, the fat and flesh and fur of the bear's back started to bubble, shimmer like the asphalt of a hot road. The bear wasn't just large, it was swollen, full to bursting with whatever it had been trying to rub off on the tree.

Jake stopped walking back up the hill, stood still and watched the bear, the corners of his eyes feeling like they would split if he opened them any wider. Jake was a smart kid, knew that standing still was not an option, but watching what was going on with the creature, there could be no thought.

Like the sunrise a few minutes prior, there could only be awe-struck observation, the taking in of a process infinitely larger than one's self.

If he was going to be run down, eaten, then he was going to be eaten by a nightmare, a phantom, not by any common bear.

The bear's back and rump seemed to shiver, elongate as it moved forward, looking like it was trying to outrun itself, get away from its tainted half.

Suddenly the bear let out a savage cry, a roar that made his previous vocalizations positively Pooh Bear-like in comparison.

And then, with no warning, the animal's front left paw buckled to the side, the bone snapping below the elbow joint, momentum causing the bear to fall uphill like its front feet had been tripped by an invisible barrier.

The bear skidded to a stop, close enough that Jake could smell the dust it kicked up. Fifteen feet away, the baby part of his brain told himself that the dust wasn't dust at all, but the smell of the animal's fear.

What was so frightening just a second ago was now so pitiful. The bear was a ruin of whining, twitching meat, no longer a threat as it lay there in the dirt.

Jake got himself moving towards his Suzuki again as he watched the bear, immobilized by its injuries.

He did not move because it seemed like he was in any more danger than before, but because he couldn't watch whatever was happening to the bear, the final throes of some deadly sickness. It could have been a parasite or some kind of infection maybe: a fast-acting gangrene, the putrification under its skin so bad that the gases trapped under the skin had ballooned, causing the animal to distend.

There was another series of cracks, a sound like the breaking of knuckles muffled by the bear's fur, and then the animal stopped moving entirely.

The bear's last sound was a slight exhalation, like he was giving up, letting the air out of his balloon. If Jake were forced to guess, pop-quizzed, then he would surmise that the bear's spine had just been snapped in much the same way the bones of its leg had.

He told himself he should turn, that it couldn't chase him now, wouldn't be offended if he beat a hasty retreat, but still he watched the body and its strange post-mortem contortions as he walked backwards up the hill.

Jake was two feet from the bike, close enough to reach out and touch the front wheels, when the bear's corpse exploded.

A mist of semi-cool blood hit Jake's face, droplets coating his shirt, but still it wasn't right. What had been inside the bear had just forced its way out, popping the animal like a zit, had somehow hollowed the animal out, drained it of the blood that should have coated Jake at this distance.

There was no time to think about it, muscle memory overrode fear, overrode disgust, overrode disbelief. It took him five seconds to mount his Suzuki Quadsport 230, four to get the key in the ignition, two to spark the engine to life in one kick, and a fraction of a second for the monster inside the bear to leap up and land on top of him.

Jake didn't have time to turn the ATV in the right direction and instead cranked his wrist as far as it could go towards himself. The bike flew over the slight lip of the ridge, going airborne just as Jake felt the pull on his helmet, the sudden sucking weight against his back.

It was on him. The monster was touching him all over his back, ripping and lifting up his shirt. Jesus did it burn.

One moment Jake Bartlett was sailing through the air, the forest floor below him, the wide bright sky above, treetops straight ahead, and the next moment Prescott National Forest was a sideways blur as his helmet was wrenched to the side.

A strong scissoring appendage tightened around Jake's neck and made sure that his head came off with the helmet.

# Chapter Eight

Even inside the car, which Kate had idling on the opposite side of the street, the gunshot was *loud*, loud enough to wake her.

Her head had been bobbing, her eyes half-closing all morning as she caught cat-naps in between stops on their route: the Merry Meth Express, making all local and express station stops at your crack den of choice, a parade of excitable tweakers chasing after the car, shouting for the ice cream man.

"What?" she asked the empty car, looking over to the passenger's side to Ken, not finding him there and then wiping a drop of drool from her chin.

As if to answer her, there was a second shot, different from the first, more of a boom than a crack. It was getting late in the day, far enough from her last high that she was getting tired and rusty despite having just woken up a few hours ago.

There were no more gunshots, but there was the sound of broken glass and then a door slamming against its hinges, confirming that, yes, the gunshot had been real and something was going down.

Kate strained against the seatbelt, turned her head towards the noise, and watched the area a few feet ahead of the car, through the windshield. After a second, Ken ran around from the back of the house. Upon further appraisal, he was not running but limping.

Kate had never seen him move so fast, his long legs able to cover a lot of ground, but his flailing arms making him look like one of those inflatable neon men that hung out outside of car dealerships.

"Start it, start it," he yelled at her and waved his hands, one empty, one full. He had the Jansport thrown over one shoulder, slipping down as he moved.

One of his waving hands was filled with, what? A gun?

Kate squinted at the black spot in Ken's fist, not starting the car and still feeling like she was caught in the strangest dream.

"What are you doing?" Ken's voice came through the window, muffled by the glass and car door. He rattled the lock. "Open up, Jesus!"

She popped the automatic locks and Ken pulled open the door, throwing his body in, not taking off the backpack but instead letting it crush between the seat and his back, probably turning a few of the bags from rocks into dust, damaged product.

Ken reached over and turned the key in the ignition for her.

"What happened?" Kate asked, not taking her eyes off the handgun. Ken had it pointed down now, the barrel lined up flush with his own knee, probably not the safest way to let a firearm rest, especially for someone who was prone to tics and twitches. Did he always have that on him? For protection? That was something she probably should have known and had never noticed before if he did.

"Huh?" he said, like he didn't hear her, an expression on his face like he couldn't have fathomed what she'd just asked. "Just drive, c'mon!"

Ken took a look back to the house to see that nobody had followed him in the trajectory he'd taken around the corner and onto the sidewalk. Ken was living out a chase sequence with no chase, but Kate pressed down on the ignition anyway, beginning to get into the spirit of things.

As Ken turned his head to follow the house as they drove away, Kate could see a trickle of blood winding from his ear down to the collar of his t-shirt, where it was lapped up by one hundred percent cotton. The amount of blood he'd lost was impossible to judge, but it probably wasn't life threatening if he didn't have a concussion.

"Can you tell me what's going on?" Kate asked, feeling herself getting more and more awake, the excitement coursing through her veins, opening her eyes but also souring her stomach. She was going to need to get high or puke.

It was one or the other and this far out in the burbs, with nowhere to safely light up, she'd probably be poking her head out the window any second.

Ken didn't turn to answer her and instead kept watch on the street around them. He was impossibly animated for this time in the day. Had he been cheating while he was in the houses making drops, sampling his wares? It was possible. He'd been able to keep the gun a secret from her, so it probably wasn't difficult to trick a pre-withdrawal Kate.

She tapped him on the shoulder with one hand, letting the car drift out of her lane as she did.

The tap caused him to jump, turn in his seat so she could see the full extent of the blood trickle. Whatever had happened, Ken was deaf in at least one ear, which explained why he hadn't been answering her.

"What happened? Where are we going?" she asked.

"Just keep driving and don't get pulled over," he said, much louder than he needed to.

He started to turn away, but she put her hand on his neck to keep his eyes on her lips, sounding it out.

"Did you shoot someone? Did you get shot?"

He lifted a finger to the side of his head. "Shotgun next to my ear! I can't hear you! Drive south."

That didn't make much sense, but not a lot about her life did anymore.

She let her fingers slide down the side of his neck, landing on one of the straps of the backpack. The Jansport was only kinda zipped and even though it was being smashed against the seat, it looked fuller than it should. They hadn't been too far along their route, hadn't had a chance to get rid of the bulk of the rocks, but there was heft to the bag now that there hadn't been when they'd started.

"What did you do?" she asked.

"Red light," Ken said, the premature age lines on his on-ly-just-thirty face becoming deep as he frowned. He'd heard her, but declined to answer.

She stopped a little shorter than she had to, the momentum of the car lifting Ken's back and ass out of his seat as she shot a hand inside the Jansport.

"How do we have so much?" She asked, her hand hitting what felt like a lot of baggies, probably three times their normal route, along with something else, something cylindrical. The revelation should have thrilled her awake, but the amount she could be roused by adrenaline seemed to have dissipated. She'd spent her last bit of energy and was crashing again.

"Drive, when we get far enough out of town I'll tell you all about it." His voice was quieter now, his hearing either miraculously restored or the yelling just an act he couldn't bring himself to keep up.

◆

"Holy shit," Ken said somewhere, maybe in her dream.

Kate started awake, her chest wet, the road in front of her passing by doing about sixty.

She'd had this nightmare before, the moments before her death playing out, the day she fell asleep behind the wheel before they could reach Rose's Tavern, killing them both.

Only it was wrong this time, she was on the passenger's side and was able to watch as the wreck on the side of the road approached. The wetness on her shirt was cooling and as she closed her mouth she realized that it was a small puddle of drool. She needed to stop doing that.

"What's happening?" she asked.

Ken had wiped most of the blood off the side of his face, but there were still auburn specks in his sideburns, so that part hadn't been a dream.

"Looks like someone had a wreck," he said.

There were no other cars on the long stretch of road. "Why aren't we on 95? Where are we?"

"One sixty-four." Ken said, slowing down and getting parallel to the back end of the car that had wedged itself into the drainage ditch. The wreck's rear tires were off the ground, with smoke curling from its tailpipe.

Kate didn't remember switching seats with Ken, but she must have done it over an hour ago. That or he'd stepped on the brakes himself, switched her out without waking her, but that seemed far-fetched. The Jansport was resting on her lap and she unzipped it to check out what she already knew. Someone else's stash was in there, along with a few rolls of twenties.

"California?" she said, trying to imply her follow-up questions, possibly failing.

Ken didn't answer, he put the car in park and got out.

Kate followed, her legs feeling weak, the itch in her shoulder blades now more of a howling scream reverberating through all of her bones, even those tiny ones in her inner ear.

As she approached the end of the pavement and gazed down

upon the wreck, she stopped worrying about California.

"We need to call 911," she said.

The driver hadn't drifted off the side of the road and bumped their head: they had hit something. The windshield and roof of the vehicle were caved in, like a cannonball had smashed into the center of the car, leaving a dent as it bounced off the hood and into the driver's face.

The white of spider-webbed broken glass was so thick that Kate couldn't tell if the driver was still in the car. The driver's side door was open, but there was no body slumped on the gravel.

"Ken, call an ambulance," she said, getting more specific this time, in case he hadn't realized she'd been talking to him when she said "we" before. Ken was the one with the prepaid cell.

"I can't," he said, pacing the strip of pavement in front of the wreck, being careful to step over the skidmarks, as if touching them would somehow implicate him in the crash.

"Yes you can," she said, turning to him, lifting his face up from the baking blacktop. "We have time, just call them and we can keep running from whatever we're running from."

"No, I mean, I can't because I ditched the phone back in Henderson."

"What?"

He scratched his neck, a gesture that made him look even more like a junkie than his teeth did. She never saw him that way, mostly because it allowed her to never see herself that way, but all the warmth that colored her perception of Ken Bowman was fading in the Nevada sun.

"The cops can like," he began, some kind of calculation or realization causing him to pause. "The police can track those things. I didn't want us to get caught before we crossed the state line."

She stared at him for a moment, hoping that the look in her eyes was enough punishment in and of itself, then she spoke.

"What exactly does that call sound like, Ken? 'Excuse me officer, my delivery man stole all my money and drugs, could you please track him with your satellites?' That is what we're looking at here, right?"

Ken's face slackened and then knit itself back up into concern. The wrinkles that had formed after losing the fat of his cheeks had made him more expressive, not less. With the paddle-boat nose and big ears, it was a cartoon face. She wanted to hit that face. To stop herself she crossed her arms against her chest. That didn't help, only made her begin counting her ribs through her shirt. How did she get back to this point? After everything she'd done to get out, for the baby, for Tommy.

*Because there was no baby anymore and there might as well have been no Tommy.*

Instead of keeping her arms on her wasted chest, instead of punching the world's worst drug dealer and stickup man, she climbed down into the ditch and walked around the wreck.

It was a nice car, or had been before its roof caved in and it had skidded into a ditch, shoveling dirt into its grill.

"Hello!" she yelled. "Is everyone all right?"

To get there, she had to step over sheets of paper that were scattered at the bottom of the ditch, the wind swirling some of them into tiny paper tornadoes without blowing them out above the walls of the ditch. The pages were typed, but marked up with a red pen, numbers in the upper right-hand corner. Someone had worked hard on these and Kate wanted to tell Ken to start collecting them up, putting them in order.

She stopped at the driver's door, and covered her mouth with the belly of her shirt. The area reeked and she could hear the buzzing of flies. Before peering through the doorway she looked up at the sky, readying herself to see a dead body, or dead bodies, and then looked.

"What can you see?" Ken asked, hugging himself even though it was probably ninety degrees in the shade.

"We need to get to a phone," Kate said, walking around the back end of the car, giving it wide berth in case it was about to shift and pin her to the ground.

"Is it that bad?" She could hear the alternate question in his voice: If it's *that* bad, why do we have to call the cops?

"There's nobody in there, which means they must have walked away," she said, the rocks and dirt between her fingers as she bent to climb up the incline feeling good.

"I didn't see anyone back that way. We should keep going the way we were headed, maybe we'll find them."

"And maybe there won't be another phone until we hit Burbank," she said and looked out into the brush and the hills. "And maybe they didn't follow the road."

She held her hand out, palm up, and fluttered her fingertips.

"What?"

"Keys. Give them to me. How far are we from 95? We'll go back to Rose's and use the phone there."

He didn't put up a fight, just dropped the keys into her hand and moved over to his seat. Kate felt awake, felt like she didn't need or want a smoke, all she wanted was to find whoever had been in that car.

A mile short of Rose's Tavern, she needed to pull to the side of the road and have a smoke.

# Chapter Nine

"One five, please go check out C-thirty-two, the alignment sensor just went off. Over," the voice on Eric's walkie chirped.

Eric pulled the radio to his lips and depressed the button.

"But I was going into Tosche Station to pick up some power converters," he said, releasing the button, waiting for a response, then remembering what he forgot and hitting it again. "Over," he added.

"What? What does that mean? Over." the voice asked, now unfamiliar to Eric.

Eric thought it was Mendes on duty today and thus okay to mess around: guess not.

Checking on the panel wouldn't be too much of a trip out of his way. Eric had actually been en route to the north station when called. They had a better vending machine there. Ho Hos were Eric's jam.

"Ten-four, will check C-thirty-two. Over," Eric said, feeling a burn deep in his cheeks that might have been embarrassment.

*Boring conversation anyway*, he thought.

Raising a hand to shade his eyes, Eric tilted his head to look down the row of solar panels, and then pivoted to read the aisle marker. He was all the way down at the double Gs. He would have to walk about four city blocks to get to the Cs.

And it was ninety-five degrees, in the shade. Maybe it hadn't been embarrassment in his cheeks, maybe that's what melanoma felt like as it bloomed on your skin.

Sweltering heat or not, Eric liked his job. He liked to tell the women he met that he made a living "Harnessing the power of the cosmos!" Or at least he vowed to use that line when he found the right woman, under the right circumstances.

A more accurate description of his job might read: Eric Iglesias, Executive Bird Gut Scrubber, as that's what he spent most of the day doing. Well, the active parts of the day, at least. Most of his time at work was spent sitting in one of the stations, waiting for a call.

The plant's automated solar panels turned with the sun to ensure the best angle for maximum productivity. Maximum surface area on the photovoltaic cells meant more energy for everyone's slot machines.

Lots of panels, lots of surface area out here in the middle of the desert, no problem, right? Well, the drawback was that the panels themselves were deliberately flimsy to account for wind gusts and were therefore easily knocked out of alignment when they weren't locked in place.

Nine times out of ten it was a dead bird doing the knocking, meaning that Eric would have to use his trusty mop to push the poor creature off of the panel before the mechanism could be reset. The heat on the panel got so intense by the middle of the day that the bird's goose was usually well and good cooked before Eric could remove it. Sometimes, when he was hungry, the birds wouldn't smell half bad and he'd end up craving Chic-Fil-A on the way home.

Dead birds aside, the job was cool because there was time to watch his shows. With no wi-fi or cell reception out in the rows to stream with, Eric would load up his iPhone with the most recent episodes of *Ninja Turtles* and *Agents of S.H.I.E.L.D.* (sometimes a few *Greatest American Hero*es, if he was feeling nostalgic) and watch the day away. He'd eat junk food and try to stay cool in north station, an earbud in only one ear in case a call came in from the walkie-talkie. If all that TV, plus some nice government coverage, wasn't enough to offset a few sunburst birds, he didn't know what was.

"One five, while you're out there, D-twenty-two needs a look, too. Over." Eric's radio buzzed, the reception on these things was crap. Two splattered birds in the same hour were rare, so were misalignments so close to each other. Eric would have to remember to add these rows to his Powerball numbers.

"Copy, will do, over," Eric said.

Reaching row C, Eric put his phone away and undid his earbud. It was irrational, but walking down a row of raised panels always gave Eric the creeps and he wanted to be able to hear his surroundings.

When he was a kid growing up in Massachusetts, he'd gone

to a farm on a school trip. It was fall, so there was a corn maze, and of course he'd been ditched by his classmates and ended up lost. The thick curtain on either side of him had been frightening, the idea that someone could burst out of the corn at any minute and *get* him, at the very least pants him.

He got the same way with in-ground pools. If they were deep enough that his feet couldn't touch the bottom, he could imagine they had sharks or barracudas swimming around somewhere in their depths. Duh-da. Duh-da. *Yeah, fuck you too, John Williams.*

Spooking himself, Eric reached to his belt for his pokey-stick. The pokey-stick was actually the mop handle that comes with a Swiffer Sweeper, useful for Eric because it came in three pieces that could be unscrewed and stored in his belt when not in use. He turned down the row, the gently curved solar panels turned almost completely parallel to the sky now, high noon.

All of them except poor old C-thirty-two, that one was doubled over, its shiny reflective face leaning against the sand.

*Fuck.*

There was no use trying an automatic reset, it wasn't going to work. So much for Eric's lunchtime Ho Hos, this panel was going to take a few hours to fix.

He tried to imagine what kind of bird could have taken the panel clear off its hinges, probably nothing short of an eagle or a seven-forty-seven.

"North?" Eric said into his walkie, pausing a moment for the dispatcher to listen to what he was going to say. "C-thirty-two has been knocked off its base. I'm going to try to lift it back up and will radio back in if I need assistance. Over."

"Copy. Over."

Copy? That was it? Okay, fuck this guy.

"Oh, no problem, you just relax and let me worry about it. Over," Eric replied, not pressing the button, letting that one stay between him, the sun and the dead birds.

Eric approached the downed panel, waving a hand in front of his nose. "Jesus!"

It hadn't been an eagle, it had been a shitbird. The front of the panel was slick with its remains, whatever it had been, and it reeked.

Propping his pokey-stick against the neighboring panel, C-thirty-one, Eric took a rag from his belt and began to wipe the panel down.

The thick brown goo did not slide off easily, but instead soaked into the rag, the viscosity seeming to firm up and go stringy as Eric pulled back his hand.

There were no feathers, no blood and no bones and as he cleaned, Eric found himself thinking of those shows about UFOs they played on the History Channel. Down in New Mexico they loved to talk about cattle mutilation and anal probes, but he'd never heard the one about the alien invasion beginning with the E.T.s jizzing on our power supply.

Once Eric used up all three rags he'd been carrying, he decided the panel was close enough to clean.

It wasn't clean at all, but if he propped it up onto its base and tightened whatever screws needed tightening, the sun would probably vaporize the rest of the space spunk and nobody would be the wiser that Eric had half-assed it.

This next part was the worst. Even though a dislocation this bad only happened once in a blue moon, Eric liked to think of it as his main source of exercise when it did happen. Not that that mindset helped any when it came to getting low to the ground and pushing the panel back up towards the sky.

He put on his gloves, cracking his knuckles and getting his arms ready for the load.

If his mother were here, she'd tell him to lift with his knees and not his back. It was a good thing she wasn't here, because Eric would have a hard time not telling her to go fuck herself. To lift with his legs meant doing a squat to get low enough to the ground and Eric Iglesias was not going to do a squat. He totally could, but he was not going to.

Even wearing the gloves it was possible to cut himself on the glass edge of the panel, so Eric dug two depressions in the dirt, enough for him to get each hand under the lip and point it towards the padded part of the glove, the meat of his palm. Where the callused part would be, if Eric had calluses.

Eric began to count backwards from three in his mind, not even lifting yet but already feeling a large droplet of sweat run over the bumps of his spine and then get soaked up by the waistband of his boxers. *Two.* He closed his eyes and prepared to strain.

He stopped before he got to one, interrupted by the sound of a crash. He turned his head and opened his eyes to see dust rise from farther down the aisle.

"What the fuck?" Eric said, wiping his eyes on the bottom of his shirt, looking up just in time to see a shadow crawl under the row on his left, row D.

"Hate to do this to you, but C-twenty-nine just went dark. What a day, huh? Over," whoever was working the radio today said into Eric's ear.

"I know, I see it," Eric said, not adding that twenty-nine was all fucked up, had hit the ground hard enough to crack. "I think you need to call animal control, there's something taking these down and it's not a bird. Over."

"What? Over."

"I saw something and it was big. Call the park rangers or something. Over."

"Nice one. You're funny. Just fix it and head in. Over."

*Never mind, prick.* This was enough for one day. They weren't going to fire him over something like this, so Eric scooped up his pokey-stick, tossed a few handfuls of dirt over the gooey rags and about-faced back towards the station.

He didn't get paid enough to tangle with whatever had been hopping along the panels. What was it and how did it get up there, seven feet into the air, not once but several times? Whatever it was, it was somebody else's job to deal with it.

Eyes forward, hands firm around his stick, Eric would return to these questions when he was safely in his swivel chair, half-eaten pastries on his desk. Now he had to get out of these rows.

It was nearly one now and the panels had begun to dip with the sun, obscuring his line of sight and turning each row into a solid corridor.

There was movement to his right. He could hear, but not see, something shuffling alongside him in row D. Or was it in E? It was hard to tell, the curved dishes did funny things to sound.

Picking up the pace, Eric broke into a light run. He was going to get some exercise today after all.

As he feared, but still kind of expected, the sounds from row D began to match his pace.

Huffing, Eric radioed in again. "Look I'm not messing around, call someone. I'm still in row C, nearing the corner!"

There was no reply. Eric wheezed and then depressed the button again. "Over, goddamn it."

"Okay. Calling them now. Over."

Although he'd been running with his eyes fixed in front of him, Eric glanced towards the sound of D.

There was nothing to see beyond the blinding reflection bouncing off the panels. The light accompanied a heat that was becoming more pronounced by the second. Eric licked his lips, felt them going chapped.

Eric lifted up the pokey-stick, slowing down as he approached the corner, out of breath.

He'd make it to the junction and would no longer be lost in the corn-maze configuration of the panels, but he'd be face to face with whatever had been knocking them down and leaving slime trails. Stopping, he asked himself if that was what he wanted.

His running partner stopped as well.

"Mendes, is that you?" Eric said, closing his eyes against the hot glare, sweat stinging his chapped lips. He needed to drink less soda, more water. "Coming in on your day off to fuck with me? Really? Loser."

There was no answer. There was also no way that it was Mendes on the other side of that panel, separated by an inch-thick layer of metal, glass and the solar conductive alginate that the company used.

Whatever it was, it had successfully jumped onto a fully raised panel before, so Eric lifted up his gaze to the sky and wondered if the animal would try it again. If it did, he'd try to skewer it or swat it with his stick before it could land.

"Come on, then," Eric yelled, stick held out like a spear, the panel bouncing his own words back at him, hurting his ears.

The attack did not come from over the panel, but from under it, the glass shattering as the mirror of the panel was tilted back up towards the sky.

The creature bashed into it from the bottom, breaking the panel inward and raining down shards on Eric's face and hands.

Eric's first thought was *Gorilla!*, but that wasn't quite right. Keeping a handle on his stick, even through the cuts that seared only a second after they occurred, Eric let fly and smacked the creature in (what might have been) its head.

Years of being picked last for Wiffle ball had done little to place a precedent for this swing, but that didn't stop it from being positively titanic.

Beneath the pants-pissing fear that the events of the last five minutes had instilled in Eric, he allowed himself to feel a moment of pride as the Swiffer rod dug into the animal's flesh with a solid splash.

"Fuck you," Eric said and threw up his hands. The creature fell back onto itself and took the stick along with it, the hard plastic and metal embedded into the animal now, so the creature would have to be buried with it.

The victory was short-lived, though, as a moment later the animal pulled itself back up, reconfiguring the bones it had already taken into its ever-expanding mass and latched on to Eric by the legs.

The creature spent the next twenty minutes digesting his flesh and pulling the majority of Eric Iglesias's bones from his body while he was still alive and screaming.

# Chapter Ten

Vicky Quail had GPS, a nearly full tank in her van, and a stomach full of Carl's Jr., so it didn't much matter that she didn't know where she was.

She was somewhere in the hills southeast of the city, probably close to the Arizona border. It didn't matter where, specifically. Over there it was desert-y, over here it was a little greener. She had a Rolodex of hunting licenses back in the van. One of them would probably keep her out of trouble; it didn't matter what state she was in.

Gambling and hunting both fed different needs in Vicky.

Gambling was all bluster. To stay competitive at the tables, Vicky would need to keep a never-ending stream of bullshit wafting out of her mouth. Playing up her pubescent-looking face and rosy cheeks, she had to convince everyone around the table that she was not a threat. To do this she called upon a quarter-century of always being the loudest girl in school, and sometimes turned the naiveté up like she was pledging a sorority, not shooting craps.

Hunting was the opposite: solitary instead of social, silent instead of loud. She was good at acting a fool in casinos, but it was *because* hunting demanded quiet and patience, not *in spite* of it, that she was able to excel. She spent all her theatricality on the casino floor, burned it up for the marks, cameras and pit bosses. She had mastered this mode as a kid too. Little Vicky would come home after a day of tearing it up at school and field hockey practice and be quiet in an effort not to wake grandma, to impress her father with how mature she could be, if she wanted to.

The rifle sat, barrel balanced over a large boulder, the stock not touching the soil, but instead resting on a terrycloth rag that Vicky sometimes used for gun oil. Through her binoculars, Vicky combed the horizon, dipped down into the valley looking for movement. There was nothing except for the soft rustle of brown grass, the hen cover. At least it was rustling the right way, telling her that she was downwind.

An antelope would have been nice, but Vicky'd settle for a rabbit. Climbing up here she'd been stopped by the soft warning rattle of a diamondback, but she let the snake be. She was not a fan of killing something when she didn't have to. She was also not a fan of snake meat. Maybe that was why she'd been bitten last year: because she let too many be. The bite didn't kill her, though, obviously, it just cost her a trip to the ER where she had to wait longer than you'd think, *no insurance.*

There was a noise beneath her on the hill, rocks shifting, but she couldn't see whatever it was while leaning behind her natural blind.

Vicky held her breath, moved slowly as she picked up the rifle. She kept her head down, checked her hat and listened. M&M red had not been a good choice of hair dye. She should have gone green, something that wouldn't look entirely foreign out here in the wilderness. Oh well, she changed it every two weeks, tucking the dye under her sweatshirt at CVS because that shit wasn't cheap.

More movement. Whatever it was, it was big and it had wandered around the side of the hill, right under Vicky's nest. It would be an absolute barrel shoot if the angle wasn't impossible, if she could lean far enough over the rocks to shoot straight down without falling off.

She gave herself a ten-count, hoping the animal would move out and away from her a bit, so she could sight it without moving positions. On eight, it did.

It was an elk, the biggest animal you could find in this area without a four-hour drive north. Vicky's heart jumped. She could sell the excess meat, the fur. The only problem would be moving the fucking thing, even to flip it and field dress it.

*Whatever, you can call a towing service if you have to, hire a fucking cherrypicker.*

She had one shot. If she didn't down this thing straight off she'd be chasing it all day.

It was beautiful, and it moved as if it were proud of its weight and knew how rare it was, at least in this part of the country. A hipster elk, moving to south Nevada before it was played out.

Imagining the beast with horn-rimmed glasses and a plaid hunter's cap made it easier to consider putting a bullet in it, imagine it as three separate coolers in the back of her van. Vicky smiled, prepared to wince once she saw the damage of an exit wound at this range, less than thirty yards.

*I'm sorry*, she mouthed and moved her finger to the trigger. Too many go-arounds of *Bambi* when she was a kid, she couldn't help but apologize.

The elk raised its muzzle and bolted as she raised a bead on it, breath still held, cheeks beginning to pinprick with red. It crashed into the brush and trees, zigzagging down the mountain, keeping in the thicker cover and not cutting across the valley, as if it had known, had aced basic elk training.

"Motherfucker!" Vicky yelled, having to restrain herself from putting a couple rounds in the sky, wasting ammunition and calling the attention of any game officer that might have been patrolling the area.

She sniffed herself, checking both armpits. Nothing.

It wasn't her jacket: the thing was lined with charcoal, brand new, still had the Bass Pro Shops security tag on it. Picking up the terry-cloth, she pushed it to her nose. Clean, no oil. Nothing in front of her nose, she felt the breeze on her face and was hit with it.

Rot! The stink of months-old Chinese food she found in her cooler that one time, the cooler she tossed rather than tried to salvage. She didn't blame the elk, she wanted to run from the scent, too.

And yet she couldn't run, she had to know what it was, had to investigate.

Thus was the duality of Vicky Quail, the perverse imp person-ified, five foot, face like a teenager, but still the girl who'd mastered the art of circumventing the porn-blockers at the library, just to see how far she could push it in public. She had a tattoo on her left tit of fanned cards, a royal flush, with the words "Fuck Your Perfect System" written underneath.

She needed to see what could smell that bad, had cost her shot, even if getting any closer to it would make her puke.

Packing her gear, planning to scrub for the day if she couldn't find a spot that didn't reek, she followed her nose around the hill. It would be getting dark soon, the sky already brushed gold, the color that told you to drink more water if you saw it in the toilet.

After a five-minute hike, she found the source. It wasn't much, kind of disappointing really, just a dead coyote.

Well, the fur, at least. A hunter must have left it, taken the meat and bones. Fucking slob. She tilted the skin back with the tip of her rifle. The stupid asshole had taken the innards with him, leaving nothing but the hide. If he packed it all together, then the meat would most likely taste like shit before he got it home. An amateur and a slob.

The smell wasn't just the dried blood, or the maggots, it was the thin layer of goo that coated the pelt. It was probably some kind of fungus, but Vicky had never seen the like. The stuff smelled, long strings of it gluing the fur to the forest floor, picking up dust and flecks of grass. Vicky shrugged and began to walk away, using the rag to wipe down the muzzle of her rifle. The rag was now toast, would always smell too strongly to be brought into the field.

The movement beside her was so sudden, the roar so loud that she barely had time to register what the crack was that followed it. The sound was a tree trunk splitting, falling, missing her by inches as the pine needles dug into her scalp, the ends of the branches scratching at the area under her eyes, the boughs feeling so heavy on her that they squeezed every cubic centimeter of breath out of her lungs.

"Timber," Vicky Quail whispered to herself before losing consciousness. Well, herself and whatever had been big enough to knock down a tree.

# Chapter Eleven

"You do get the occasional channel cat, but it's bass mostly," the old man said. "Both large mouth and striped," he added.

What was spectacular about him, what impressed Marsha the most, was not that he'd lost his entire arm below the elbow, had it bitten off, apparently, but how damn calm he was about the whole thing.

"You think a fish did this?" she asked.

"Well doc, I didn't really get a good look, with the blood and everything, but you've seen the animal network, what that British fellah pulls out of the water?" he said and pointed to his stump. "Well…"

"A Loch Ness monster?"

Abe was pale, but most seventy-five-year-olds that came in were. This one had spent most of his retirement up to this point fishing the Colorado River.

"Nah, just a big fish, 'tain't no monsters in there. If there were I'd have caught one before this. The Mohave is deep and not far from where I was set."

This was her second time hearing most of this. The colloquialisms seemed to have shifted since last time and the man had stopped taking gasping breaths, grabbing at his stump. He'd told the attending about it last night, then her this morning and now again when she'd gone to check on him. It was possible that he didn't recognize her when she'd reentered the room, the amount of morphine in his drip.

Abe was monopolizing her time. Even first-year residents didn't spend this long with a single patient. The way the hospital was set up it was usually no more than five minutes a shift per patient, max. Some of the stable patients on the floor never got checked on by a doctor, if nothing was changing in their treatment.

But Abe was exciting. Not only was it pleasant to hear him

talk, but he'd had one of the strangest injuries Marsha Roberts had ever seen.

"Weird. It hanging around in a junk pile like that. Just goes to show you how nature adapts: man pollutes and ruins and most animals just don't give a fuck, just keep on going, using the environment they're given. Pardon my language, hon."

"You should hear what people say in here," she said. Usually, if a patient called her hon, or asked her how old she was ("you look like my granddaughter!"), or confused her with a nurse, the mistake would send a chill of righteous fury through her. But Abe Martin got a pass.

"Am I going to feel it later on, like a phantom limb?"

"It's possible, but we shouldn't worry about that just yet. Let's just look towards discharge, then you'll be meeting with a physical therapist."

"If I hurt my phantom wrist, I'm guessing I don't take Advil for it," he said and smiled, his question just a setup for a dirty punchline.

"No, you wouldn't," she said, parrying his joke with an actual answer. "You've taken this remarkably well, to be able to joke about it."

"Just the kinda guy I am, I guess, never look on the…" He stopped mid-sentence, looking past Marsha to the door.

"Dr. Roberts," called an unfamiliar male voice from behind her.

Marsha turned at her name, the unfamiliar voice belonging to an unfamiliar face.

"Excuse me, but I need to talk with your patient," the man said. He was in his mid-to-late thirties and wore a blue sports jacket over khakis, his outfit screaming golfer. The worst kind, the one who golfs in the desert, demanding fresh greens dripping with dew in a climate that wasn't built for it, using up precious water.

"I'm an agent with Fish and Wildlife," he said, hooking a thumb at his own chest, sensing that he was being sized up.

*Whatever, that doesn't mean he can't golf in his spare time.*

"Can I get a moment with Mr. Martin?" he asked.

"Of course," she said, not looking for a fight, no real reason to keep listening to Abe spouting his personal philosophy about the attitude with which one should face life's little setbacks. Amputation by fish, for example.

"Abe, the good news is that I'll see you tomorrow. We need the beds, but we don't need them that badly. We aren't letting you go just yet," she said to the old man.

Abe nodded, like being cooped up in the hospital was inconveniencing him, looking like he couldn't wait to master the art of one-handed fishing, maybe from the riverbank this time.

Three hours later, as she was getting ready for sign out, two and a half hours after his discussion with Fish and Wildlife, Abe Martin was pronounced dead of heart failure.

# Chapter Twelve

Nez awoke to a smiling female face, which was strange because he lived alone.

It was a nice face, but it had seen better days. The girl had bloody teeth and smooth skin between the pinpricks of new scabs. She knocked on the truck window and shouted at him.

"Hey, mister! Just checking that you're not dead," she said, her frame short enough that her mouth couldn't reach over the door to the window, the top of her head wobbling like she was on tip-toes as it was.

Her high voice drew him fully awake, and fast. He looked around himself, studied the gearshift, put it all together that he had finally fallen asleep behind the wheel, but took solace in the fact that he'd been parked at the time.

"Sun's up," she said. "You're going to cook in there."

Nez checked his watch. He tried to remember how many sick days he was allowed. Two sounded right. Shit.

He rolled down the window, looked at the girl who even though she'd claimed to just be checking on him, wasn't going anywhere.

"What happened to you?" Nez asked, not sounding as concerned as he wanted to, but he'd just woken up, wasn't in the best of moods.

"I was crushed by a tree. And almost eaten, I think."

Nez laughed, watched as the girl dropped her arms from the exaggerated shrug she'd just put on. She had big eyes, bright red hair and a tank top that nobody's grandmother would approve of.

"I'm serious. I was hunting and," she lifted up one hand, made a cracking sound with her voice and tipped it over, "boom."

"Almost eaten? By a bear?"

"More like bigfoot. Something that big and that fast? Total cryptid territory. I only saw a shadow, would have seen more if I hadn't been under a tree at the time."

"Do you need a ride to a hospital?"

She blinked at him, looked behind her to the van parked parallel to his Ford, then up towards Rose's. "No, I have a ride. I need a drink."

Nez pointed to his own temple, and then nodded to the driver's side mirror.

She looked into the mirror, dabbed a finger to her tongue, then rubbed it along the side of her head, not getting the blood completely off, more like applying rouge.

"It's worse than it looks, that's all scalp-blood. No major arteries or shit like that, just little nicks."

"It's probably not open," Nez said, looking towards Rose's, squinting against the sun and trying to tell if the neon was lit or not, amazed that the Zima sign still worked at all. He rubbed the top of his head, wondering if his hair looked okay after sleeping. He liked to keep it buzzed, but if he went a few weeks without a cut it would stop looking cop-cool and start standing up. It was strange that he was caring what he looked like. It appeared as if the girl had just been beaten, and she was only a little more than half his age.

"Nine forty-five on a Saturday. Wanna bet?" she said, a glimmer in her expression that told him she wasn't kidding.

Nez looked around the empty dirt parking lot, then caught the glint of a hubcap and bed of a truck from behind the building. Someone was in the bar and they'd left their truck in what could be jokingly referred to as employee parking.

"I'll pass on the bet, thanks."

"Wanna beer then?"

"Yeah, sure. I've got to use their phone anyway." He put his hand to the ignition, took his keys out without having to turn them, thankful that he hadn't left the engine on for the night.

It was so easy to say yes to the beer, because it meant human contact, even if the human looked like a hardcore streetfighting Keebler Elf. He rarely drank, but still wondered if he could keep up with this one, all hundred and ten pounds of her.

He followed her across the lot. She had a heavier tread than him, like she had something to prove, and was kicking up dust clouds with every step.

When they reached the door, she grabbed the handle and paused. "Whatdya think? I think I hear a jukebox."

She pulled and the door opened. The lights were on, but that jukebox must have been her imagination, because it was silent in the barroom.

"Wiseass."

"So maybe it was my internal soundtrack," she said. If she weren't so cute these would all be red flags. Even before whatever they were going to drink, a year ago Nez would have made her walk a straight line before letting her get back behind the wheel of her van.

The bartender was staring at them, his eyes blocked by the sun's glare on his thick glasses.

"After you," Nez said, wanting to get inside and close the door, aware that they were letting the cool air out.

All the time he'd spent parked outside the building, Nez figured he'd have had a better idea of the layout of Rose's Tavern, or at least know what the bartender looked like, but he was wrong.

The bar was nicer than he'd guessed, smelling like polished oak and stale beer. Nez had imagined dollar bills tacked to the ceiling, maybe a sheet of sawdust and peanut shells on the ground, but it was more like an Irish pub than a dusty roadside bar. Sure some of the upholstery on the stools had seen better days, but the lighting was better than average, the glasses strung up above the liquor bottles all looked clean, even the martini glasses that probably saw infrequent use.

It was strange that they were the only patrons. Bars like this normally had at least one fly hanging around.

"Morning," the bartender said, pushing the word out from under his thick white mustache. He was not rude, but did not seem happy to see them, the odd pairing they were. Cop-vision and bartender-vision were likely tuned to similar frequencies and Nez guessed the pair of them looked like trouble. If not trouble, hassle, at least.

"Fair morrow, my good sir," the girl said, bowing. "As you can see, it's been a long night and I am parched and weary."

"Two Buds," Nez said, getting the words in as she took a big theatrical breath, the barkeep giving him a raise of the eyebrows that was both "thanks" and "is she for real?"

The girl frowned, telling Nez that he had pissed on her parade, and they took seats at the bar.

"I'd ask for your ID, darling, but you've got a head injury, so," the bartender said, seeming to warm to the girl as she leaned into the bar, her camouflage tanktop dipping. Her lips were glossy and as she spoke this close to him, Nez could smell cherries.

He looked, the bartender looked.

"Thanks, sugarstache. Does your wife leave you alone with the grandkids?" she said, her voice hardening, threatening the old man not to look at her breasts even as she presented them. Cute but not without the capacity for cruelty, Nez would remember that.

"That'll be five," the bartender said to Nez, averting his eyes.

Nez paid. "Can I get quarters for the phone?"

The girl swiveled in her seat away from the bartender who moved off to go mess with the register. "So what's your name" —she gave a fake cough—"champ? You see I paused there because I almost said 'chief', but I didn't because I realized at the last second that that would have sounded racist. I'm always hyper-sensitive to stuff like that."

"Thanks…it's Nez. Um, or David. Do you always talk like this or should we be worrying about a bleed up in your brain?"

"No, this is pretty much constant," she said, swigging. "I'm Vicky Quail, thanks for asking, you're a real gentleman. Quail like the bird, not the ace reporter from Gotham."

"Sorry, I didn't…"

"Just fucking with you, Nez. Oh look, pool."

She pointed beyond Nez, upended her beer into her cherry-scented mouth, and jumped down from the stool.

"You play?" Nez asked, which seemed to be a given at this point, the way she was chalking, circling the billiard table like a pint-sized predator.

"Yeah I play. Did you ever shoot anyone in the line of duty?"

"Jesus. How did you know?"

"That you were a cop?"

"Yeah." *Sure, that.*

"You look like one. Also I peeked in on you while you were sleeping, remember? There was a Navajo Nation jacket in the seat next to you. You haven't made detective, I'm guessing," Vicky said, racking the balls up, making more noise than she had to. Nez glanced over at the bartender, still playing with the drawer on the cashbox, but his head tilted to listen. Things probably didn't get much more exciting for this guy.

"Won't ever. I'm not a cop anymore."

"That's a relief. It means you can't arrest me for the savage beating you're about to take. I'll break."

And she did.

"Solids," she said, announcing the obvious and then sinking two more before it was his turn.

Nez wrung the cue in his hands, examined his options, and then excused himself to call in to work.

He went to the corner of the bar, the half-open door of the bathroom smelling like bleach, and could feel her eyes on him. He got an answering machine, which at a call center was fairly ironic, and told it that he was ill and wouldn't be in today.

Nez returned to the game and reassessed the table.

"I would go for fourteen, in that pocket, but that's just me." She pointed and then asked, "Want another beer?"

He hadn't even seen her finish hers. It was kind of miraculous, her getting the liquid into her mouth between all those words so quickly.

"I'm all set with this one," Nez said. "Thanks."

"Teetotaler. Figures. You *totally* shot someone," she said, walking backwards into the bar. "Jack, neat."

At least she didn't talk while he leaned over the table, lining up his shot. She had that much restraint. Nez poked out, scooted the ten into the corner pocket, deliberately ignoring her bum advice. She was good, but all that glitz was covering something, an insecurity maybe, a lack of competence. He'd be at the eight ball in two more turns, minimum.

The bartender poured her drink and then slid the bills out from under Vicky's chipped nail polish.

"Thanks, salt-n-peppa," she said. The nickname was for his mustache, Nez guessed, since the guy had obviously dyed the hair on his head: a ratty-looking ponytail. The bartender's pale skin was turning red. The girl was succeeding in getting to him.

Vicky drank her whiskey over one and a half turns, sipping not shooting, and was calling the eight while he still had the twelve on the table.

"That one," she said, pointing with her cue and putting an ungodly amount of backspin on the ball so it didn't go a millimeter farther than it needed to sink into the pocket. It was impressive: she may have been hiding insecurity, but she had competence to spare.

"Well, that's it for me I think, I gotta get back out there. Get back on the trail."

"Out where?" Nez asked, pulled closer by Vicky's words than he wanted to be. Something about the girl didn't feel safe.

"About ten klicks south." She held out both hands in front of her and made right angles with her thumbs and forefingers, the way a grade schooler tells the difference between left and right. "East, southeast of here. To catch that thing."

"Catch it? The bigfoot?"

"It's not a bigfoot, per se, I was just making a…" Vicky said, her words trailing off, turning thinking into a show, like she had made a show of everything else. "And I don't really mean catch it-catch it, that's a euphemism. I mean that I'm going to shoot it, repeatedly."

"Permits?"

"All up to date, I swear. Officer."

"Then I guess I can't stop you."

"You want to?" she said. There was a flirtation there.

"Not really, but I don't want you getting killed, either."

"Eaten?"

"No, passing out in the hills from a subdural hematoma and dying of exposure."

"I knew you didn't believe me," she said. "Don't much care." She did.

Nez stuck out his hand. She shook it, wavered a bit, a lightweight not because of low tolerance but because of physiology. There simply wasn't that much space inside her to put the alcohol.

"Be careful driving," he said.

That was when the tweakers busted through the door.

# Chapter Thirteen

Grant might have puked last night, or he might have ended his bender with an especially wet burp. Either way there was debris in between his teeth as he woke up, brushed aside the soiled sheets and walked to the bathroom.

The motel sink was built for midgets. With all the money he sunk into this place, they still couldn't be bothered to change out the ancient fixtures or throw some new grout up. He bent over the basin to slurp at the dirty trickle of water, his hair catching on the faucet as he swished and spat.

The motel was quiet, though. It was even quieter since the ice machine had broken, with the hookers pulling stakes long before that. The good ones getting themselves a check-up, a receipt for the check-up, and heading to Reno. The bad ones migrating to Vegas, the sleazier part.

It was quiet enough to write. He'd published before, under a pseudonym, but that wasn't the problem these days, the problem was finding quality markets for *real* literature.

L.A. had nearly killed him. Not physically, because that death was still happening by the handle, but emotionally.

*Here's some money, write this screenplay that we don't intend to make, but hey the money spends.*

If he was being honest, getting paid wasn't the problem. The problem came when he stopped producing the non-scripts. It was hard to put your heart into something that maybe three people were going to read, two of them interns who were going to have to fill out a little grid while they skimmed through his hard work.

*Compelling characters? Three out of five.*

He'd never seen one of those completed cover letters for his own scripts, but he knew they existed. And that they existed put him into a neurotic frenzy as he wrote, had him writing for barely employed USC grads instead of a movie-going audience, or himself.

So he'd fled. Not far, about half a tank of gas away, but far enough that if he looked out his motel room window it was practically a moonscape.

Nobody used this road anymore, so nobody used this motel like a motel in the traditional sense, for a one-night stopover. Grant wasn't the only Los Angelino ex-pat using the Starbright Motel as a flea-bag condo, paying by the month so the maid could ignore him for most of it.

He walked over to his computer and woke it. Next to the laptop he had a small inkjet printer, an accordion file, a case of ink cartridges and three blocks of cheap Staples-brand printer paper. Excepting his clothes, his car and a stack of second-hand books, these were his only belongings.

After a few clicks of copy-paste magic, the inkjet hummed and he poured himself two fingers of Cutty to drink while he pulled on pants and a shirt.

Finishing his drink, he added the freshly printed (*mmmm, warm*) sheets to the accordion file and headed out the door to go to work.

The Acura used to be a thing of beauty, the kind of car that was conspicuous when it showed up in a film because it looked too much like product placement (which it most certainly was). *Used to be* a thing of beauty. Grant drove it less than ten miles a day, but the desert had caked it, looked about to crack it, even when he was sticking to the highway.

Grant liked it better this way, he wasn't getting on any studio lots with it looking like that, but it was exactly the ride for a struggling novelist. The car was his old life: encased in dirt and fossilized so he could create.

*But still with an element of class, dashboard GPS standard.* He smiled and popped his locks.

As sober as he would be all day, Grant opted for the less trafficked roads so he could open up the V8 engine, new for the 2015 model. His accordion file was on the seat next to him, his book his only and favorite passenger. Write drunk, edit sober. More than just a funny Papa quote, it was a way of life for Grant.

Well, "write blind, edit while drinking" was closer to the truth.

He had ninety thousand words burning a hole in his hard drive (and his Dropbox account, natch), but only about half of those were usable. He would type up his corrections when he was ready, but for now they stayed in the accordion file, a solid three pounds of marked-up printer paper that he brought back and forth to the bar with him.

Driving out here was a different art entirely from driving in L.A. Fuck traffic, there was no traffic even if you were headed up to Vegas.

Out here your vision could be panoramic, life in Cinemascope, as long as you glanced forward every minute or so to scan for movement, either in your lane or coming the opposite direction, if you were drifting over a bit.

Which was exactly what was happening when he saw it, running parallel to him.

His initial reaction was to slow down, get a good look, but once he looked he dropped the pedal to the floor. The rush of movement did not remind him of a car chase, but something older, a western where the lead cowboy was preparing to jump from a moving train, his trusty horse panting to keep pace.

They were pushing eighty, and *this* horse was having no problem keeping pace, its strong legs pumping, its elastic flesh rippling as the air pressed against it, like skin under a leaf blower. It wasn't a horse, though, it was bigger.

If you went down to San Diego, then went a little farther to Tijuana, there were more than a few knick-knack vendors that would sell you a stuffed jackalope, and if you spent enough time on the internet you'd see articles about chupacabras running loose by the TexMex border. But the goat-suckers were just dogs with bad cases of mange and the jackalopes were taxidermy rabbits with deer antlers stuck to their skulls. The thing, the cheetah-buffalo keeping pace with Grant's Acura, was real.

Backing the hum of the engine (which wasn't loud, that's part of what you paid for), Grant could hear the creature huffing with exhaustion. It was the kind of sound that a dog made bounding after a tennis ball, not explicitly happy, but the emotion implied by the listener anthropomorphizing the animal's breath, its jowls pressed back in a mock-smile.

Grant screamed to nobody, the sound buffeting the windshield.

Curving his body he scooted down in the driver's seat like maybe if the monster couldn't see him, it would lose interest and stop its pursuit. But he couldn't get low enough and still wanted to keep an eye on the creature to see what it was doing.

His heart jumped, feeling like maybe he'd won, as the creature began to creep back, parallel now with the back window instead of the front door. But the lag was just it climbing up the ditch, getting closer to the car until it was padding against the pavement behind him.

If Grant slammed on his brakes he could hit it, but would he kill himself in the process? People died all the time, crashing into deer, but this was a fuckload bigger than any deer. Taking one hand off the wheel, two for just a second, Grant buckled up.

The creature was fast and mean-looking, with all those bones jutting up through its skin, a face made of bone, it seemed like, but it didn't look especially solid. He could cream it with his Acura, back over it if he had to, once it was down.

"Okay you fuck, prepare to be front page news!" he shouted. It seemed like something one of his characters would say. One of his old characters, the ones in the screenplays-for-hire, never the characters in his novel, where naturalism was king.

*Dialogue? Two out of five.*

He took his foot off the accelerator, balanced it over the brake, and a twinge of hesitation was all it took to ruin his plan as the animal sensed the slight deceleration and took all four of its feet off the ground, leaping on top of the Acura, landing with full force with its front legs, caving in the windshield and roof as the car skidded off the road.

The airbag punched Grant in the nose with a force that, if he hadn't been wearing his seatbelt, would have shattered his face. As it was, his nose was probably broken. It felt warm as he touched it with his pinky.

There was steam but no smoke, which was good as it meant he wasn't about to explode.

Grant flattened the airbag with his forearms and looked out the smashed window. He couldn't see much beyond the wall of the ditch.

"Gross," he said to himself as a glob of foul-smelling fluid dropped on him from the divot where the roof met the busted windshield.

If that was blood, it meant that the creature was probably

hurt, had probably been thrown off the top of the car when it had stopped so suddenly. Grant smiled: car beat monster, rock beat paper.

Grabbing his accordion file from the passenger's side floor, he took his phone out of his pocket and opened the door. He was able to open the door all the way, the cherry on top to what couldn't have been a better high speed crash.

Did he call 911 or animal control? he asked himself, squinting against the sun (the Acura's windows had been treated, just a light tint), and peeking over the edge of the ditch. There was a long brown stretch in front of the car, not only dark from upturned dirt, but from the ooze. It smelled terrible.

The greasy landing strip was satisfying, but where was the body?

Next to him, the Acura groaned, the front wheels making a quarter turn, the back end of the car slamming down so the trunk was propped up by the dirt, not the asphalt.

Grant looked north, at least he thought it was north, it was the direction the car had been pointed and he didn't think that they skidded a complete circle so that his sense of direction had been switched. There was no monster.

Looking back over the car, there was also nothing.

He wanted to shrug, begin his ascent to the side of the road and his (probably long) wait for a ride, but he *needed* to see the thing, to know it hadn't been the weirdest, slimiest pink elephant ever witnessed by an alcohol-pickled brain.

Grant got his wish as the limb lashed out from under the car, splitting as it wrapped itself around both his legs, pulling him down. There were those visible bones again, but some of them had been shattered, sharp splinters playing against his jeans, making little, audible tears at the denim as they tried to work the fabric apart.

He screamed "No!" as the Acura rose up slightly against two wheels, the creature freeing itself from its hiding spot, what had to be a hiding spot because it had been tossed clear of the crash. Grant had seen the path of overturned rocks and dirt.

The probing limb(s?) had split his pant legs, seemed not to care about the inorganic matter, just wanted his flesh and bones, a live meal. The creature rolled itself thinner, casting a shadow but going see-through as it stretched itself impossibly huge over Grant's body, like a living wave cresting over him, ready to crush him.

Inside the wave there were patches of fur, hair, teeth, animal and human all mixed up. *Soon I'll be in there,* Grant thought, still clutching his accordion file.

He needed to make his last moment count for something, throw his work free of the creature, so it wasn't digested too.

Tossing the file up and over, trying to make it to the asphalt, Grant sobbed as the creature smacked it out of the air, denying him the final peace of knowing his work was safe. Not only that, the thin elastic tie that kept all the pages together broke, scattering them to the wind as the creature began pulling off his legs, working its way inside of his bowels.

The intensity of the desert sun faded as the creature finally descended on Grant's mouth and eyes. He caught his last glimpses of the world, his manuscript blowing in the wind, as if through a window comprised of brown, ugly stained glass.

The liquid flesh of the monster burned his eyelids away, digesting them, letting him know that soon, there would be only his bones.

# Chapter Fourteen

The door creaked in its frame, someone pushing instead of pulling, and then the two junkies fell in, the metallic burn of meth smoke heralding their arrival. They straightened up, trying to compose themselves and failing.

Vicky felt an instant thrill upon seeing them, like they were a ten-point buck standing in a field of knee-high grass.

It was hunting season.

The guy had been the one struggling with the door. He was tall, considering his tower of unkempt hobo-hair: the man had a few inches of height on Nez. The male junkie had prominent features made even more prominent by his sickness, like a cartoon character after a few rounds of radiation. His eyes weren't as all over the place as the woman's were, though, so it was possible the smoke wasn't wafting off of him. Maybe he'd only gotten a second-hand buzz.

The junkette started to speak, but couldn't get words out, wheezing like she'd just run a marathon. Through the green-tinted windows of the bar, Vicky could see that there was a new car in the parking lot, parked between her van and Nez's pickup. The woman's run couldn't have been more than a fifteen-yard sprint. *She'd probably be in better shape if she wasn't hitting the pipe*. Vicky read in an article somewhere that drugs were bad for you.

"Oh never mind, let's not leave yet, I want to stay and watch this shitshow shake out," Vicky smiled and non-whispered to the cop, Nez.

If the junkie woman heard her and took offense, she didn't show it. That was a bummer. Vicky liked riling these people up, it felt like getting back at her mom with none of the late-night guilt or psychological baggage she normally associated with lashing out. Vicky's fixation on her fucked-up mom would probably break her down to a sobbing little girl if she ever stopped counting cards and shooting wild-life.

"Benny, we need to use your phone. There's been a car accident on I64," the woman said, her irises completely invisible, pushed to a sliver by pools of black.

Vicky turned to Nez, ready to ask who the fuck Benny was, but then the bartender spoke.

"Nine-one-one is free on the payphone."

The woman began a hobbling run to the phone, still winded and hitching up her backpack, leaving her traveling companion alone so he could belly-up to the bar.

The couple lent credence to Vicky's thesis that you always saw junkies in pairs. They were like Turtle Doves. Leaning against the front of convenience stores, passed out on the bus, arms curled around her step-father like a boa: junkie bugs in a rug.

All this thinking, ruminating, was upsetting her perfect day. Why the hell was there no music in this bar? Vicky hated silence and made it her mission to tear it down.

"Wait," she said, turning around to face the bartender who'd begun pouring something cheap for the male tweaker without being asked. "You're telling me your name isn't Rose?"

The bartender didn't acknowledge the joke, just slid the piss lite-beer in front of the seated junkie.

"You believe these two, Ken?" Benny, if that *was* his real name, said to the junkie.

The man had to turn on his stool to look back to where the bartender motioned, the expression in his eyes telling him that he was noticing Vicky and Nez for the first time.

"First my morning regular doesn't show up, which means he don't buy his beers and to-go bottle, then you two are late, and I'm stuck with an Injun and one of Santa's helpers as a fuckin' consolation prize. A beer apiece. Then they make like they're gonna leave and don't."

The junkie looked preoccupied but gave a hollow laugh when Benny was finished, like he hadn't heard or understood what was said but sensed that there was a punch-line, then sipped his beer.

Vicky never would have guessed their new bartender friend harbored such strong feelings.

"That's fucking offensive," Vicky said, taking a few steps to the bar. Nez reached out for her shoulder but she dipped under and away.

"Leave it alone," Nez said.

"Some of my best friends are members of the Elvish coalition. And I had a whiskey, too. Overpriced."

"Look missy, take your tits and your annoying fucking voice out of my bar," the old man said.

"I don't know, maybe five miles south. The car might be hard to spot… South of us, I told you, we're at…" The woman tweaker had to repeat herself to the operator, her voice getting frustrated. Stringing directions together was probably tricky when you were tripping balls.

"I'm going to climb over there and rip that Wilfred Brimley dick duster off your ancient fucking face," Vicky said. She'd actually thought of the Wilfred Brimley crack over twenty minutes ago, but hadn't had occasion to use it. Good thing Benny had spoken up, or the joke would have never fit.

She took a slow step as Nez dropped his arms around her, pinning her fists to her sides. The cop reacted exactly like she thought he would.

Vicky wasn't really going to fight the bartender, she just enjoyed making grand entrances and exits. Nez's arms were strong and he smelled like a guy who'd just spent the night sleeping in his car, which wasn't an entirely bad thing.

"Hello? Hello," the woman junkie said, the frustration boiling over into panic in her voice. Vicky's mom used to have episodes like this. One time she'd been trying to paint her nails, her fingers not cooperating, and she'd retaliated against the world by setting the kitchen on fire. That had been the 911 call that earned her dad an extension on his shared custody, so in a way it was a happy ending. More time with her dad, watching movies.

"They hung up," the woman said, jolting Vicky to the present. *Shit, sometimes junkies made her nostalgic.*

"Emergency services don't hang up on people," Benny said, not taking his eyes off of Vicky. Nez wasn't moving her out the door, was just standing behind her, still holding on.

The junkie asked if anyone was there, pecking at the receiver with her fingers, the clicks seeming to echo, the closest thing to music Vicky had heard since the van's radio this morning.

"Phone's dead," she said, sounding on the verge of tears.

Vicky chanced a look away from the bartender, their fight simmering, fading, but the adrenaline and Nez's forearms wrapped around her still feeling nice.

"Goddamn it, Kate, the phone's not dead, you're just high and stressed and at least your ear is not still ringing!" The guy, Ken, had finally spoken, addressed the world around him.

"Wait," Vicky said, the words catnip to her, but not focusing on the obvious question, about why the guy's ear was still ringing. "You guys have, like, almost the same name."

The lights in the bar cut out, the room going dark, the windows letting in very little light between the tint and chicken-wire.

"Kate and Ken, foreva," Vicky giggled to herself, repeating the names. Nobody else seemed to think it was funny, they were all more concerned with what was going on with the power.

*Bunch of pussies.*

# Chapter Fifteen

Benjamin Shea hated being reminded of Rose. Which he was every day, coming into work, but the reminder was rarely out loud, and never came from someone as obnoxious as the pixie with the bright dyke haircut.

Benny also hated that he'd never bought a weapon more lethal than a citrus press to stock behind the bar. He hadn't ever needed one, had only broken up a handful of fights in twenty-five years, but rolling a baseball bat over the girl's ribs would have felt really satisfying right now, in the darkness, before heading out to check on the generator.

He wondered how much trouble the Indian would give him if he tried anything. The tall skinhead was cut, held himself like he could have been military, not slouching even when he had been sitting at the bar. Benny would have taken his chances, nobody ever expects much out of an old man.

He wondered if Kate and Ken would back him up. If it meant they drank for free, they would help him bury the bodies, whistling the whole time, if it went that far. Drugs were a scourge, but not a scourge that was going to drop away from society anytime soon, and, at least in Benny's experience, tended to lower the moral threshold of most addicts.

Not that Benny was a killer, at least he hadn't been yet. Rose was the reason he wasn't, why he didn't have that bat, or a sawed-off shotgun, tucked under the bar, lying across the top of the kegs.

Back when they'd signed the deed, she wanted the tavern to be a homey place, had even wanted to call it an inn. Benny had to draw the line somewhere, though, so it was a tavern. A nice compromise between the roadside biker bar he'd envisioned owning and the Prancing Pony of Rose's flower-child imagination.

It didn't much matter what they named the bar. After the state had redone the highway system—had found a more direct route to Vegas—the tourists had left their business behind. Rose had lived to see the change, which was two more years that Benjamin was lucky enough to have spent with her, but they weren't the two best years. Those two were the years of no business and grand mal seizures.

"Did you pay your electric bill?" Ken asked, his voice a rasp, like he'd been crying. What was up with this guy? Usually when he came in, he was all smiles, kept talking about payday. And why did half the people who'd walked into his bar today have head injuries? There was a dark circle of dried blood in Ken's ear, now even more apparent in the low light.

"Brownouts happen. They used to happen more. I've got a generator, one second," Benny said, feeling his way to the back door, using the shelf behind him for support, his movements rattling bottles of tequila that nobody ever ordered, being just for show at this point.

The power outage was a pain in the ass, but in a way Benny was thankful for it. He wasn't the kind of guy to count backwards from ten while punching a pillow. All of his softness had come from Rose, had been *for* Rose, so with her gone he was an angst-filled teenager again, knocking over mailboxes because he felt like it and it wasn't as illegal as burning down houses.

"Need help?" the Indian asked. Okay, duly noted, he was a nice guy, and didn't even seem to know the girl he'd walked in with that well.

"I've got it, it's one switch. Weren't you two on your way out?" Nobody responded, the girl giving a sharp intake of breath that Benny took to mean that the Indian had somehow stopped her from speaking.

Benny opened the back door, letting the light pour into the bar, then stood on the threshold before moving forward, listening. There was no movement behind him. Ken was so deflated that he hadn't even tried to lean over the bar to the taps and refill his beer. That was very much unlike Ken. Maybe something was really wrong, maybe whatever accident they'd witnessed had shaken him up more than he wanted to admit. After the power was sorted, maybe they could all take a ride out there, before the police showed up.

He put his mind to one task at a time and stepped through the back door, out into the light.

The sun tried its best to burn you the second you were outside.

It was like it didn't want people here at all, had claimed this section of the country in the name of Sol. Benny had soaked the rays up in his youth, his Harley between his legs, leather cut on his back (but not his arms or shoulders), but that was before he'd met Rose and swapped chopper rallies for peace rallies. Then they'd sunbathed together, sat out on courthouse steps with a purpose before he'd talked her into wising up and selling out, owning a business. They'd opened the tavern, an oasis for weary travelers, and begun to see less of the sun.

The damage was done at that point, though: the sun had turned Benny's skin into toughened leather. Not that he'd completely disliked the look, but it had taken a bigger toll on Rose. He switched the bike for a car with UV-treated windows, after that.

Gravel shifted under Benny's boots as he made his way out to the generator, a separate wooden shed behind the bar, his car parked at an angle in between the two structures. As he walked he looked left and right, east and west, checking to see whatever was wrong with the electric, if it could be spotted naked eye.

The prime suspect would have been storm clouds, but there were none today. The poles stood tall, stretching as far as he could see to either side. He could not hear the cicada hum of the capacitors. The power outage was likely caused by the heat. The NVE built these conductors and transistors as tough as they could, but Mother Nature always found a way to cook them, overload them, and Rose's wasn't located in a high traffic enough area to justify digging an underground network.

*Or maybe they've just shut off the electric so you dry up and blow away. To hasten the inevitable, old man.*

It wasn't just a quiet day in the bar, but outside as well. There were no birds overhead and the wind was non-existent. The day was completely still. The only movement was the illusion of movement, waves of heat dancing off the hood of his car.

Benny reached the door to the shed and stopped. He looked down and contemplated the combination lock for a moment. "Fuck," he said aloud, the hair of his mustache brushing his bottom lip. His whiskers had gotten long enough to be annoying. He would have to trim them soon.

He stared at the lock. They'd had it for close to a decade, but he always jumbled the numbers up in his head. He knew what they were, well, two out of the three of them at least, and could remember that they went in some kind of order, either ascending or descending.

The first few times he'd forgotten the combination, Rose had joked that he was losing his marbles. The next few times after that she'd just frowned and recited the number, making him repeat it back for her before he went outside to unlock it. They'd both been thinking it: he was old enough that dementia wasn't out of the question. Over the years it became less likely as it became apparent that Benny could remember everything *but* the fucking combination. After that it had come full circle back to laughing about it, Rose hiding the combination from him so he couldn't cheat and look it up without asking her for it.

He wished that she'd told him where it was hidden, before she'd gone away.

With one hand twirling the wheel of the lock, hoping something about it would jog his memory, Benjamin Shea baked in the desert sun.

All the numbers were double digits, and the first one definitely had an eight in it. Now was it eighteen or twenty-eight?

There was a sound, in the distance, a twang like a broken guitar string. Benny had his eyelids pushed shut, the numbers right at the tip of his memory, and had to fight the instinct to look towards the sound.

*Twenty-eight.* Then what? *Twelve.* That was the easy one, Rose's birthday, January twelfth.

He opened his eyes. He could cheat on the last one, dialing the wheel back slowly while he pulled the lock down, letting it pop by itself, no number required.

There was the sound again, not exactly the same, more of a thundercrack this time, maybe it was a storm that had knocked out the power.

He looked southwest towards it now, where the road went on into infinity, disappearing only when it met the horizon.

The poles holding up the power lines were falling like dominoes. Something massive was pushing against them, the shape moving parallel to the road at great speed, using the lines like a squirrel would. The thing was too heavy for the lines to support though, so they snapped beneath it like baker's twine. Before its bulk could touch the ground, it bounded up into the sky, higher than any animal could jump, where it then crashed down on the next pole, catapulting itself onto the next. This maneuver sometimes snapped the pole, sometimes left it vibrating like a cartoon diving board.

Benny stood agape for a moment, and then looked back at the bar, to the short distance he'd have to traverse if he was going to make a run for it, then looked back to the generator door, pulling down and the lock undoing with a satisfying click.

*Three. Duh.*

He opened the door, rusty hinges squealing, and closed it behind himself.

The room was only big enough to house the generator and one person. Beside the generator was a propane tank and a half-full gas can, the gas last topped off when Bush was in office. Not the son, so it was possible that the can's contents were nothing but dust. Above him, hanging from the ceiling like the world's least cutesy mobile, was a collection of tools.

There was light to see all this by because none of the boards were flush with each other, the sun beams cutting through the four by three box in dusty lasers.

Outside he could hear the shattering of telephone poles continuing, the pace not slowing and the sound getting louder. Benny's brain had hardly enough time to reconcile a world where the existence of the creature was possible, but all the same he found himself thinking: *Please don't let it have seen me. Please let it keep going, not slow down.*

Although he didn't want to, would rather have just listened to the thing pass, Benny could not stop himself from pressing one eye up to the gap where the door met the frame. Peering out, he was able to see half of the bar, a thin line of asphalt from the road and the two nearest poles.

There, pressed against the door, his breath held, Benny felt a drop of urine hit the fabric of his briefs and spread a circle of warmth about the size of a quarter against the front of his underwear. Pushing his eye as far as it could go, he counted each impact, begged the creature to keep going, passing his bar.

When it landed on the roof of the tavern, he felt a strange mix of dread and relief. He didn't want to die, didn't want the monster to wreck his bar and kill two of his regulars, but if it were a choice between that and the creature hopping onto the shed…

It paused on the rooftop, almost like it knew it was being watched, allowing itself to be taken in. Although it had just jumped thirty feet, had to have been going over forty miles per hour to get there, the creature was not winded. In fact, it didn't appear to be breathing at all. The only movement of the thing's flesh was a gentle drooping downward as its joints relaxed.

What had been coiled muscle a moment before was now resolving itself into a waxy sludge, losing all momentum and the surface of it liquefying, like butter in the microwave.

Its bones shifted inside it, a mass of ribs stretching itself flat and peeking over the side of the building, a periscope or a blind man's cane, feeling its way around the lip of the roof, looking like it was seeking prey.

The sight atop the bar was unreal, massive, but it did not have the fluid unreality of a dream or a hallucination. Benny tried worrying at the edges of his short-term memory, just to see if there was any way the sequence of events didn't add up, that this was his imagination.

*Oh yeah, I was running a fever, doing Jager shots, watching Steve McQueen in* The Blob *by myself when I tripped and fell into to bed and then...*but he had no such luck.

Having seen enough, Benny closed his eyes and brushed the sweat from the top of his head, running his hand back along his long, thinning hair and closing his fist, the perspiration styling him a temporary ponytail. If the creature was planning on wrecking the bar, he didn't think he could bring himself to watch.

When he opened his eyes again, the thing was gone. No, not gone, he could still see the appendage reaching over the side of the building, testing the shuttered back windows. It had just stretched itself thinner against the lip of the roof. It was big, but it wasn't big enough to Saran Wrap itself over the sides of the building and trap all the patrons inside of its mass.

Benny put his hand into his pocket, felt the keys there and eyed his car. He'd parked it at an angle, the driver's side door almost perfectly aligned with the door to the shed. He could make it in less than twenty seconds, about as long as it would take him to open the door to the shed, the door to the car and then close it again.

Running his finger over the automatic lock, the black molded plastic of the key, he thought about it. He also thought about whether the animal would be able to see him, or if it sensed movement, or if its vision was ultraviolet or if it could hear really well or if it was attracted to the smell of piss. There in the darkness, Benny took stock of all the monster movie conceits.

It was as good a time as any, while it was occupied, before it jumped over to investigate the shed. Hand on the door, Benny took a step back and prepared himself to run.

And as he did so he tapped the rusty gas can with the back of his foot, the sound echoing, containing all the subtlety of a cymbal dropped inside a library.

The creature picked itself up off the roof, resolved itself back into its firmer shape. The bones turned at impossible angles in their non-existent joints, building themselves into a new alignment. The monster was biological jazz, its skeleton a shifting, freeform structure.

The creature jumped, higher than it had to, the air time giving Benny an extra half a second to dive out the door and fall into the scalding dirt, a cloud of dust flying up into his mouth that burned not only as it whipped through his nostrils but settled into his lungs.

A moment later the shed was gone, crushed under the weight of the thing, a weight that must have been tons, even though it moved like lightning.

Benny turned over onto his back, kicked away with his feet as he watched the creature climb out of the wreckage. The bones had moved around to encompass the shattered remnants of the shed, broken boards with rusty nails poking through the creature's midsection, impaling it. Along with some other detritus, the bent exhaust pipes of the generator became porcupine quills out its back.

There was a brief moment where he thought the beast had killed itself, recklessly jumping down onto a structure that could not possibly support it, but then it moved. It pulled its flesh from where it had puddled against the busted generator, slapped against the small concrete square of the foundation.

Benny got to his feet, his wrists and knee howling, his legs spinning under him so fast that for a moment he thought he would fall again. He caught himself, though, used the nose of the car to find his balance as he looked up to the back door of the bar.

Ken was there, his eyes wide, the door cracked open far enough for his face to stick out. Benny raised a hand, waving for help. Ken didn't offer any, but mirrored the motion, raising his own hand and then curling all the fingers but one inward, pointing behind Benny to what he knew was coming, to what gripped him under the arms, gently, tenderly and lifted him off his feet.

For about three seconds, Benjamin Shea was airborne, ascending fast enough that he could feel the whiskers of his mustache pulling flat against his lower lip, the wind pushing against him.

As he crashed back down to earth, the phenomenon was remarkably similar to diving into a pool at an expensive resort. You wanted to take in all the sights around you, but you also wanted to get the initial shock of the cool water over with. The air around him blew by, the world bright enough that he could pick out individual sheets of tar on the bar roof below him, but then they'd passed over that, had jumped completely over the tavern, were going to crash down in the parking lot. Instead of water, they crashed down into the desert, Benny's consciousness pushing through the ground and, without hearing the splash, into a cold, dark world.

# Chapter Sixteen

It was only a minute ago that Benny had left them alone in the darkness, but already Kate was making friends.

"There was nobody around, no other cars and no broken glass on the road. I think something bad happened to the driver," she said to the two strangers, the line of reasoning that Ken'd heard multiple times in the car. The guy was feigning interest, but the pixie girl's eyes were beginning to glaze.

He knew what Kate was doing, she'd done it before and would do it again. When she smoked she got contrite, started explaining herself and her mistakes to anyone who would listen. Now she was explaining to these two folks why she had needed to use the phone so badly, that they were on their way to Los Angeles when they had found the crash.

Ken never saw the point in justifying his actions aloud. He was going to do what he was going to do and hopefully it would be the right thing. He *did* try to do right.

Ken sipped his beer, realized that he had only a few mouthfuls left and decided that he would have to slow down, ration them until Benny returned to pour him a new one. He would sometimes pour his own, goad the bartender into a Sylvester and Tweety interaction, a play fight that would always result in him paying for the beer, even the stuff he spilled, but his heart wasn't in it today.

Shooting someone and being shot at tended to put a damper on things.

It wasn't supposed to go like that, it was meant to be a stick-up. A stick-up where everyone except him was high, a sure-thing that would result in a nice retirement fund, a nest egg for him and Kate to get clean with. He hadn't consulted her, but it seemed like the type of thing she'd be into. Getting clean, that is, not holding up the money guy.

He realized now, wetting his tongue with the disappearing beer, that the large man with the shotgun had likely always been in the kitchen, every time he had come to exchange drugs for money. Just because he'd never seen him didn't mean that the shotgun man hadn't existed, and not planning on his existence had been junkie logic. Ken really did need to get clean.

The big man, stone sober and probably bored out of his mind, had been listening to Ken's exchange with the skinny guy who'd then tossed him the paper bag of cash. It made sense, now that he'd had a chance to think about it, that there would be a professional on the scene at critical junctures like this. Not taking security like this into account was the reason Ken wasn't a stick-up man.

On the bright side: the gun Ken bought had worked. It was a shitty nine millimeter. Whoever had filed off the serial numbers had gotten a little overzealous and had given the metal a rough finish, like the gun had been sitting in a drawer full of steel wool for the last decade. The guy who'd sold it to him had pushed in a fresh clip and showed him how to switch the safety on and off, told him to squeeze, not pull, the trigger, which was something that Ken had heard in movies.

Ken had walked into the shitty track house, sweating through his shirt, but that wasn't a giveaway. He was always sweating, it was in the high nineties and he was a drug addict. He exchanged pleasantries with the skinny guy, the guy he'd always seen planted on the couch, tossed him the baggie, watched him reach under the couch, pull out the paper bag of cash.

Ken pulled the gun on him.

"All of it," Ken said, not raising his voice, but still trying to get some menace into it.

The skinny guy frowned, then smiled, a reaction that Ken chalked up to whatever the guy'd been smoking to stay so skinny.

Ken took a step forward, then another until he was close enough to take a seat on the couch beside him. Keeping the gun on him, he bent and picked up the paper bag, feeling the weight of the cash inside.

The man with the shotgun was huge but moved like a shadow. Ken hadn't noticed him until the coolness of the barrel pressed up against the back of his head.

"You're dead, motherfucker," the man said, just a voice then, before Ken had seen him. Ken believed him and in one twitchy moment decided that turning and firing was his only choice to maybe get out alive.

Ken led with the pistol, firing before he was completely out of the way of the shotgun's blast and catching the man high, in his shoulder, the nine pointing up as he redoubled his grip on the paper bag, feeling it tear underneath his fingernails.

The shotgun was a white blaze of light and static as it fired next to Ken's ear, knocking the glasses off his face.

It was over just like that, no thrilling choreography, no Saturday matinee heroics, just two guns going off in close proximity to one another, both spatially and temporally.

The man with the shotgun fell back, giving up his grip on the weapon, no longer caring about the money as he moved a hand to cover the hole in his chest.

Ken was deaf, unsure if half his face had been blown off by the blast. After a moment of feeling his own breath he concluded that it hadn't. There was no time, and no real reason, to attempt to scoop up the glasses. They weren't even his right prescription, just some drug store readers he'd picked up to hold him over until the next time he remembered to pick up his contacts.

He scrambled for the door, and as he started to fumble with the latch on the screen, he turned back to see that the skinny guy was the only one not walking out of this. Ken had once known his name, but it was long forgotten. They'd settled into a routine and lately he was simply the second guy on Ken's route, no name needed. Now the guy was one with the couch, having caught the full blast of the shotgun at the right angle and distance that most of his head and chest were gone, particles of bone and flesh dripping off the opposite wall.

Even before he was around the front of the building, yelling for Kate to start the car, Ken had begun to ask himself just how culpable he was for that man's death. Whether he'd hang for it or be gunned down from the people he was stealing from. Whether the death of one junkie demanded the blood of another.

In the car, Ken had resolved to tell Kate about what had happened once they'd crossed the state line. It would be tough to explain, how he'd thought it had been a good idea at the time, but she deserved to know why they were running.

Then they'd found the crash and she'd wanted to turn back to

Rose's, and Ken agreed. Well, not that he agreed, not that he still didn't want to get as far from their normal routine as possible, but because a beer sounded good and there would be no stopping Kate's neurotic complaining until they found a phone.

And he wouldn't have to explain the gunshots until they crossed the state line.

"I'm Kate and that's Ken."

Underneath the constant white noise of his still-ringing ear, Ken heard his own name. He used a finger to probe the tender flesh inside his ear and the tip came back brown and flaky. And blurry. Maybe he needed those glasses after all.

His ear might have sustained permanent damage, but it would never be as permanent as the damage done to the skinny guy. Or the couch, for that matter.

"Are you just chatting us up to use one of our cell phones, Kate? Because if you are, I don't have one. I don't like being tracked down," the girl with the red hair said, making a show of the contempt she seemed to hold Kate in. Ken didn't understand how someone could brag about not having a phone, not in this day and age.

Kate started to stammer something, but the Indian saved her.

"I don't have a phone but I've got a radio in my truck. It works, I think."

"Thank you," Kate said. What a hero this guy was, or at least wanted to be. On any other day Ken would have liked him, but not now, not today. "Do you want to come, Ken?" she asked, turning on her way out the door with the man.

Ignoring the question, Ken looked up at the lamps hanging over the bar, expecting to will them on with his mind. He should have joined her and smoked when Kate pulled the car over. He'd been worried that it would have made him even more high strung, but now he realized that there was nowhere to go but down.

"I wonder what's taking him so long to turn the fucking lights on," Ken said, finishing the beer in one swig. He turned in his seat to look at the group.

That's when he heard it. From the looks on their faces, the first glimmer of interest in the pixie's eyes, they all heard it too.

Kate started to say something, but Ken stood up and shushed her.

Distant cracks, each a few seconds apart, like the felling of trees. But that wasn't right, because there were no trees anywhere near the bar.

"What is that?" the girl said, a weird happiness in her voice, as if the events of the last ten minutes had bored her and she was once again waking up.

Ken hadn't considered the darkness of the bar anything other than an inconvenience a second ago, but now it frightened him. None of this could be connected to his crime, could it? Irrational fears, the kind that he hadn't felt since he was a child, began to press on him from the gloom.

"Fuck this," he said, moving to the bar and ducking under the back entrance, where only Benny was allowed to tread. Following the sunlight, he turned into the small storeroom and approached the back door. The heavy door had been left open a crack by a wooden jamb.

Ken looked out just in time to see Benny, visibly shaking, remove the lock from the shed and close himself inside.

*He's only just now opening it up?* Ken thought, but was interrupted by a bang and a cloud of dust floating from the ceiling. Something had crashed down on top of the bar.

"What is it?" Kate asked, touching his shoulder at the same time, her sudden appearance an unhappy reminder of the last person who'd snuck up on him today.

Through the boards of the shed, Ken could see Benny, the whites of his eyes at least, the bartender looking up to whatever had landed on Rose's Tavern.

As Ken made out these details, he was relieved to find that at least his long range vision was fine. He remained only farsighted. And partially deaf.

"I don't think we should stay here," Kate said, and Ken shushed her. The noise in his bad ear was no longer indistinct, but was instead the sound of his own blood pumping. Between the tentative gentle thuds from the side of the building, Ken imagined that if it became quiet enough he could hear the synapses firing in his brain as he tried to think, a starter that refused to catch.

"What is he looking at?" Ken asked. As he did the door to the shed flew open, Benny diving for his car and falling flat on his face, an unfunny *America's Funniest Home Videos* blooper.

Dust rained down on them again and Ken moved to the door, taking his weight off the doorjamb and preparing to help Benny.

Then the shed exploded and Benny was on his feet and trying to run. The thing pursuing him stood about as tall at the shed had been and moved on two legs, steadying itself with a third that appeared to form from nowhere out of the bulk of its body.

Ken let the door get heavy against his arm, ready to close it, trying to make his face an apology to Benny. But then it didn't matter because neither Benny nor the creature was on their way inside.

They were on their way up.

# Chapter Seventeen

Nez would have liked to credit his training for being able to predict everything that Ken, the junkie, the perp, was going to try to do, but the fact was that it was obvious.

No police academy sleuthing required: Ken was set on leaving the safety of the bar and no amount of reason was going to stop him.

You could see it in the way he'd called the woman, Kate, over and opened up her backpack, pulling out a baggie the size of Nez's fist—clearly more where that came from—and then fishing a pipe from one of his pockets.

He was lighting up a bowl for good luck. Or courage. Or both. Luck and courage for his great escape.

The bulb of the pipe glowed orange and then went dark again. Ken was silent for a moment, let tendrils of white smoke escape from the sides of his mouth, seeming oddly calm as he did, then whipped himself back into a tizzy before he spoke.

"You didn't get a good enough look at it, man. It's the size of a fucking Buick. Bigger!" he said, the glass pipe still bobbing from his lips, smoke curling away from his words. "You want a hit, babe?" He offered the pipe to Kate, who looked back at Nez and Vicky and declined. She wasn't one to imbibe while in mixed company, Nez guessed.

"We gotta get out of here, right now, while it's gone."

"And how do you know it's gone?" Nez asked, wishing he had his notepad, if only as a prop for questioning this guy. If you write the occasional word down, make it seem like a deposition, it changes the whole tone of any conversation. Especially if one half of the conversation was grinding its teeth into paste.

"If it were up there, we would still hear it." Ken motioned to the roof, no longer creaking under the weight of the animal like it had been a minute ago. "And if it were out there," Ken said, stabbing his fingers towards one of the small front windows, "we would see it. Believe me."

It was hard to tell what they had seen in the parking lot, the two members of the group that had gone to the back door and got the best look were…unreliable.

Vicky and Nez had gathered at one window, the junkies posting themselves at the other while Benny was being attacked. The windows were small and covered in chickenwire, the angle was wrong, and Vicky's van had been obscuring most of the action from Nez's view, but one thing was for sure: the thing had eaten—absorbed—the bartender.

The point of impact, where they had touched down in the parking lot, was now just a red splotch on the packed dirt. There were scraps of fabric glued to the ground, a small pile of wet laundry, and nothing else.

When the thing was finished eating, the process taking about five minutes, the beast had moved itself out of sight, crawling low to the ground, towards the hill to the northeast. Its movements were sluggish, full of Benny-meat.

"It knows we're in here. If we don't get in our cars now it's going to knock down that fucking door the moment it feels like a snack."

"And once you get in your car?" Nez asked. "We don't know much, but we know it's fast. Or at least it can be. Could be around the side of the building where we can't see," he said, thinking of the snapped poles, the ground and air it had been able to cover.

"Well," Ken said, his eyes fluttering to indicate that he was thinking meth-quick, but not yet ready to vocalize his ideas. "We've got three cars, at least two of us will make it."

Vicky laughed. "We're safe inside and you're already writing a carload of us down in the loss column? We should play cards some time." She punctuated her statement by muttering "idiot" to the quiet room.

Confrontational as she was being, she was also speaking sense. Nez was in her corner, had held her back from starting a fight with the bartender, but it was getting awfully hard to defend her as she goaded Ken. She looked like a sweet kid, a regular strawberry shortcake, but there was so much bitterness left in the fruit.

"Yeah? Well, that's not all," Ken said, looking to rebut her. "I've got a gun in my car."

Now Vicky laughed again. There was meanness to it, but also genuine entertainment this time.

"Would you knock it off? Be nice," Nez said, turning to lock eyes with Vicky, even in the gloom able to see her expression slacken, stunned that she was being reprimanded. He held on to her a little longer than he had needed to before. He hadn't done it consciously, she'd just felt nice and it had been a long time since human contact.

"It's just funny 'cause I have guns too," she said, the words coming through a puffed-up lower lip, little-girl-wounded. "And they're a shitload bigger than some crusty stickup pistol."

Ken seemed to bristle at something Vicky said, but his woman stepped forward.

"That's good, right?" Kate said, hope in her voice. Nez could see she was a natural mediator, found himself wondering whether she had kids or not. Then wondered where they were now if she did, whether or not DHS had stepped in yet. They probably should, probably had.

Ken stopped pressing his face up against the window and turned to them. There was a pale bloodless divot in his forehead from where he'd been resting it against the sill. "We need to go!" he hiss-whispered, "Now's our chance."

"It killed a man, a man much bigger than you. Before it did that it jumped, or flew, straight over the building," Nez said, pausing for emphasis. "This calls for a better strategy than running into the open and hoping for the best."

As he spoke he moved away from the two women, closing the distance between himself and Ken while trying to keep his voice tinged with the calm of a hostage negotiator. There was no reason to agitate the man any more than he had to. "Especially because we have no idea where it went. Remember what I said: it could just be waiting on the side of the building, or around the back."

He had to stick to that point, make sure it was making its way through the clouds of smoke seeping deep into the folds of Ken's brain.

"So we wait for it to get hungry again?" Ken was close to Nez now, too close, picking-a-fight close and he hadn't cooled any. The man's mouth stank, it was a rusty industrial smell like his throat was a kitchen sink, recently Draino'd. "Not happening."

Ken dug into his pocket, pulled out a set of keys that Nez could hear but not see. He wasn't going to drop Ken's gaze and risk the sucker-punch that he could sense creeping up. These people were unpredictable.

"You're driving, right?" Ken said, looking beyond Nez and tossing the keys to Kate. She didn't catch them. She barely got her hand close and they hit the ground, sliding across the hardwood.

"Oh hell no! You want to go out there so bad then you go yourself," Vicky said. She held a protective arm over Kate's chest, flitting between who she liked in this room at whim. "You don't get a valet. No reason for her to die with you."

"Maybe we should wait. Just think about this," Kate said to Ken, her voice a quasi-apology for allowing herself to agree with a person who only a few minutes ago had been holding her in complete contempt.

"Fuck it!" Ken said, knocking by Nez. "I'll call for help at the first gas station I hit." He walked over to one of the high-top tables and bent down, feeling for the keys, his palms slapping the floorboards in the darkness.

Nez looked to Vicky. He wanted to ask her what she thought, whether this was the okay thing to do, let Ken risk his life by allowing him to try this.

Judging by her silhouette, her expectant, aggressive crossed arms, Vicky was not having the moral dilemma that he was. She maybe even looked forward to Ken's chicken run. *Maybe other people were entertainment to Vicky*, Nez thought and it made him regret enjoying their embrace.

After what felt like an inordinately long time spent slapping the hardwood, the keys finally tinkled in Ken's palm and he rose up from his hands and knees. He then cursed as he bumped his head on the underside of the tabletop.

Ken rubbed his scalp, his greasy hair sticking up at a new angle, his slim profile looking like a Calvin Klein model's in the low light of the bar, his crystal-sick body not the key-light grotesquery it would be out in the desert sun.

Ken approached the door, reaching out for the knob, slow enough that Nez guessed there were second thoughts flying through his mind, the small sober part of him wishing someone would hold him back, but the addict pushing forward, ready to lash out if anyone tried it.

"Here goes," he said, adjusting the key ring in his hand, the black plastic hilt of the car key between his thumb and forefinger. He looked back to Kate as he turned the knob, stopping when he'd gone all the way but not moving the door yet.

"Take care of the bag, Kate. Don't leave it behind. Don't wave it around any cops when they get here."

Kate nodded in the darkness.

"I'll be right back, love you," he said, so quick it was all one word for Nez to decipher as he opened the door, the sunlight reflecting off the sand and dirt, filling up the bar and blinding them all.

"Do you see that?" Ken said, before running out the door, waving and screaming, Nez's eyes not yet adjusted to the light.

# Chapter Eighteen

Three years ago, Officer Dan Hammond didn't own a cell phone and was still running Windows 95 and Internet Explorer on his home computer.

It may seem impossible now, but back then he was happy with this inferior setup.

That was until the department had top-of-the-line laptops installed in all of the squad cars, and suddenly, now that setting up speed traps could be fun, Officer Hammond felt the need to become a computer wizard.

The laptops came with the internet locked down and all the good functions blocked, everything except for Solitaire and Minesweeper, but those could only take you so far as you baked in your car, the police band silent, waiting for a driver to come over the horizon so you could point your radar gun at them.

So Dan had to learn how to make alterations.

Now he was using his phone as a hotspot for unmonitored internet, running two operating systems, able to switch between them if he needed to run someone's license plate.

His phone bill wasn't so bad. It had only taken him one month to learn his lesson and buy all his data upfront. He'd even been able to dispute that first charge to his credit card, blaming it on his teenage son using the phone, AT&T flinching when he'd threatened to walk his business over to Verizon.

Now he had three tabs open in his browser (which was Firefox now, natch, although he had dabbled with Chrome), Pornhub (paused, video buffered, just in case), Netflix and Ultimate Poker.

Dan Hammond was sixty-two, had survived two wives and three minor heart attacks, and was now plugged into the web like a kid a quarter of his age. He was an old dog with the newest of tricks.

Before this golden era, he'd been counting the days until he could retire, but now he wanted to stay on the force until he died. If they would let him, he would die in his sleep peacefully at the age of ninety-seven, all-in with a full house in his virtual hand, aces and eights, behind the wheel of a cruiser.

Yes, he had to do work sometimes, but out here the quotas were so low that he only bothered with tagging the cars that were visibly cruising over a hundred, their fiberglass frames vibrating like if they turned three degrees, the car would be airborne.

Going that fast, he would have to be quick to catch them, of course. He'd nose out of his hiding spot a full mile in front of them, siren blaring. If he was feeling especially ballsy (and if not much was going at the poker table), he'd pull across both lanes, traffic permitting, forming a one-car roadblock.

There was always the possibility of getting dialed up on the radio, but all of his hotspots, his speed-traps, were usually far away from the real action. By staying in low-traffic, non-residential areas, he was never the closest officer to any wrecks or domestic disturbances.

No. After putting up with a career filled with shit-kicking and an unspectacular personal life, this laptop was Dan Hammond's just reward.

Check. Check. Bet. Lost.

There went five bucks, only half of it his, because the casino cash-matched his first (considerable) deposit. He pushed his chair away from the virtual table for a moment to compose himself.

He tabbed over to the porn, played a little further. Boring part. Then clicked over to the TV show he'd been watching (well, listening to, really). It was something his son had insisted he watch. Some space show with robots and shit. He wasn't quite following. Next weekend he'd have to read up on it using Wikipedia, make sure he at least had the characters' names down before he and the kid had dinner together, just so they had something to talk about. *They sure as hell weren't going to be talking about girls,* he thought and frowned.

He turned up the volume on the show, listening to characters bark about FTL drives and toasters with only one earbud in so he could hear any cars approaching.

The speeders almost uniformly came from the west, their souped-up engines blaring, the young drivers planning a long weekend in his state. He was ready and more than willing to get their vacation off to a shitty start, maybe send them back to L.A. for good. Hung over and bankrupt, they never seemed to speed on the way back to the Left Coast.

It wasn't an engine that snapped his attention away, but the radio.

"Seven-four, come in."

Dan sighed. One downside of the tech revolution was GPS trackers in all the cars. If dispatch was radioing him directly, it meant that he was close enough to whatever the problem was. Shit.

"Seven-four here, what you got for me, darling?"

"I'm not your darling, seven-four. We've got a 911 hang up out by you. Number's for a bar, Rose's Tavern on the old…"

"I know it," Dan broke in. He didn't need directions.

"Well the caller reported an accident but didn't say where. Can you swing by and see if you can find her?"

"I'll check it out." Dan removed his thumb from the radio, unmuted the porn and said: "Darling."

When he was finished, he switched off all his entertainment and drove in silence.

He glanced at his watch as he pulled the wheel around. It was quarter to five, the sun would be disappearing over the horizon in about an hour and he'd be off shift. This thing would probably take him through until then, if it didn't take him to overtime.

It was fifteen minutes of highway driving before he spotted Rose's in the distance, then another few until he turned off onto the old highway, dust-blown with disuse. He didn't notice what the debris was he was driving over until he'd already begun to turn up Rose's long driveway.

The road had been littered with splinters, the telephone poles on the side of the deserted highway laid neatly on their sides, some not-so-neatly spanning the ditch between dirt and highway.

The fucking road crew had quit whatever it had been doing (chopping down the old power lines?) without cleaning up after itself, without even laying out some cones. It was some real Chernobyl shit and Dan wondered how long it had been left like this. The owner of Rose's was probably ecstatic about the eyesore.

The shadows of the cars stretched long in the parking lot, but the intensity of the sun had still not changed in any noticeable way, Dan pulled further up the drive.

The bar was offset from the road by a long stretch of packed dirt, then a sparsely populated parking lot, the unlit neon sign at the mouth of the drive the only indication that there was a functioning business here. Not that it was going to attract anyone anyway, nobody used this road anymore. His windows down, Dan listened to the silence. There was no wind, no honky-tonk floating out of the bar, only stillness and the crackle of his tires.

Dan had been to Rose's a few times, back before he'd sobered up, when he'd needed a quick midday pick me up.

But no more of that shit. And not because he'd found God or went to AA, either, just because cardiac arrest was the cosmos telling you to knock it off with the 3:00 p.m. Jack and cokes.

There was no sound except the crack of gravel under tire as he pulled up behind the van, slowing to park. That was until the door to the bar flew open, becoming a black square in the sun-bleached façade of the bar.

*Why were the lights off?*

"Help! Help us! Call someone!"

The tall, skinny guy ran out of the door, waving his arms and yelling. He bobbed and weaved, his tread unsteady, looking like he was zig-zagging out the door into the parking lot on purpose. Dan felt acid rise up in him, recognizing real fear on the man's face and his mind immediately jumping to the images everyone had seen on the news: deranged men and kids with sniper rifles and automatic weapons, opening fire in public places, all because Suzy snubbed him for the prom, or they saw it in a movie or some shit.

"We're being attacked," the man shouted, huffing, his face capillary red and purple.

The skinny guy had almost reached the first car, fumbling with the keys in his hand, before looking back towards the bar and nearly losing his footing.

That's when he looked up and his yells turned to shrieks. Dan tried to follow his gaze, but with the sun setting behind the bar, he could not see what crushed the man, only hear it.

# Chapter Nineteen

Felix did not know where he had come from, how he had gotten there, or that his name was even Felix.

All Felix knew was that he was hungry.

Not that he knew the word *hungry*, which is not to say that hungry was even a direct translation for what he was feeling, but that was the closest word we have.

As the sun set, the rays no longer pelting down on his body like they had this morning but the cool desert night not yet arrived to chill it, Felix felt better.

Cooling after feeding, having taken in a meal much larger than a jackrabbit or a pike or a coyote, Felix felt good enough to stay in one place. There was now less effort needed to keep himself in one piece and he could relax, take in his surroundings, his body slowly slackening, but not dripping or diminishing.

Felix could now focus on the large puzzle box in front of him, and the food, the shrieking, scratching, whispering food, that he could sense inside.

He'd tried to crush the box, had built up a large amount of momentum jumping off the pole, but it hadn't worked. Then, sitting on top of the box in the full heat of the sun, feeling himself melting without inertia to keep him solid, Felix had settled on the one morsel he could catch.

The box was solid on the top and solid around the sides. But there was something to be done that didn't require a massive amount of time and energy. So while the food inside communicated, argued, Felix pressed himself flat against the side of the box and pushed. He could feel a piece of grating strain and expand under his mass.

It didn't hurt, detaching a piece of himself, but he did mourn for the loss of the small glob of matter. He used only the smallest bones, the thin, hollow bones of an owl, to give this construction mobility, and then the short, sturdy bones of an adolescent human's hand for weight and structure.

He slipped the bones into the thin ventilation grating, taking his time, careful not to sever his connection with the flesh until he was absolutely sure that the bones could function on their own.

When it was done, when Felix could feel his creation moving on its own, constricting spindly bones to propel itself through the vent like a snake, he disengaged from the wall, giving the piece full autonomy.

Then he *heard* it.

Well, there's that abstraction again, that descriptor that didn't quite line up. He "heard" the man running from the front of the box, screaming, but really he "felt" it. Was buffeted by the sound waves, his liquid flesh bending and vibrating, picking up the man's footfalls the same way that he was also picking up the rattlesnake, curling and thrashing as it swallowed the mouse a hundred yards to the south. The same way Felix had "heard" the police car crushing splinters, turning onto the drive a few moments ago while he was busy squeezing into the vent.

His bones shifted in anticipation. This was attack formation, for lack of any better term. Flea construction with a dash of house cat. The leg bones of six different kinds of animals moved to where he needed them, his flesh constricting, forming hardened muscles as he flexed, the pressure so great that marrow squeezed from bone shards, an unexpected boon of nutrients he hadn't yet ingested.

He leapt over the box, catching sight of the man just as the man did the same. He'd been too excited, overzealous in his jump and would not be landing on the man. That was, until the man stumbled and Felix felt himself course-correcting mid-jump, flaps of skin on both sides of his mass opening up like wings, his body too heavy to fly, but not too heavy to displace air and fall with a little grace.

Joy wasn't something that Felix felt, either, but satisfaction and exhilaration were both ballpark terms.

He crushed down on the man, the human's body so tall that his legs buckled and snapped like matchsticks, bowing outward at the kneecaps. The man's skull had been lined up with the force of the blow so that Felix's weight drove the man's head down into his chest cavity, his scalp a fuzzy mound atop his shoulders now.

In the distance, the police car skidded to a halt, the gravel and dirt of the parking lot loose enough that a cloud of it dusted Felix's hide.

It had all gone so well. Until the burning began.

The plan had been to crush the man flat, then hop over to the hood of the car, smashing the windshield and pulling the policeman out of the hole, still screaming.

But the man underneath him was tainted somehow. Felix spun to get away from it with a sensation very much like pain coating the places where Felix had made skin to skin contact with the newly lifeless body.

Frustrated and scared, Felix curled in on himself, rolling backwards away from the man's spoiled blood trying to scrape the layer of skin off of himself that had already begun to absorb the man, Felix's digestive fluids betraying him, the fiery anguish spreading, consuming over half of his surface area, sinking in deep.

That's when he felt the tugs against his flank, bullets entering him, slowing, and exploding out the other side. One bounced off a femur, split it and sent the pieces helicoptering inside of his gut.

The policeman was out of the car and firing at him.

# Chapter Twenty

Vicky opened the door just in time for a bullet to zip past her and through the room, breaking a bottle as it crashed into the bar.

Fuck, almost out of the woods, almost rescued, only to be killed by friendly fire. That would have been a disappointing way to go.

But the windows hadn't provided a good enough view, the angle not right to catch all the action. And Vicky Quail wanted, needed to see that action.

Yes, it had been horrific to see that poor junkie accordioned like that, and she felt for Kate, the woman formerly known as the junkette, but still, on some level, that motherfucker knew what was going to happen, they all did.

Screaming bloody murder for the cop probably didn't help, hadn't been the most tactically sound decision. Ken had made a target of himself.

But the diversion did stop the cop from being eaten before he could radio for help. He did radio for help, right? Vicky could only hope, she hadn't been paying attention to the cop car until the cop had dove out and begun opening fire.

The pop of the nine millimeter stopped and Vicky edged out the door, trying to get out of the line of fire before the cop had reloaded and racked.

The creature kept corkscrewing, turning in on itself like it was trying to pull a cartoon disappearing act, eating itself until it was a black hole. But this was the real world and it was beholden to the laws of physics, if not the commonly held precepts of biology.

The exit wounds were closing themselves up, the ripple marks cutting through its semi-translucent body like it were an organism made only of bones and ballistic jelly.

She could see the policeman now, stepping forward with his grey eyebrows knit into a look of concern, maybe gun-range concentration, his clean-shaven mouth an invisible line. She imagined he'd clenched his jaw so hard that he was tasting blood. Vicky got like that sometimes, feeling that fear that quarry could take a wrong turn as you bore down on it, could hook an antler up and through your pooper. It happened, not often and never to her, but she knew that sometimes the deer won.

"Get away from it," he shouted and Vicky realized how close the creature's backflips had brought it to her. It was like staring into a lava lamp, its oil-and-water undulations hypnotizing, especially for a big game hunter.

"Move back," the cop said. It sounded like one of his stock lines, like he was comfortable using it while clearing the scene of an accident so it was the first thing to float to his lips right now, with normalcy fleeting. He slapped his hand up under the butt of the gun, steadying his aim and smoothing the new clip home all in one fluid motion. It was tough to tell if it was him or the hardware, but it got Vicky hot.

He was old, but Jesus fuck if he couldn't rock and roll. If he got them out of this, Vicky was ditching good old David Nez and swapping him out for a man of action.

Vicky sidled against the front of the bar, approaching the far corner, her back to one of the windows.

Another couple of shots planted, perfectly center of the critter's mass. It would not have been easy to hit, considering how much it was flailing. A bullet pelted the dirt, another took a bite out of the doorframe. The cop's face got redder, and he looked like he hadn't taken a breath since stepping out of the car, seventeen, now eighteen bullets ago.

There was another change in the thing: it crouched down low, hardening as it folded its layers back into itself, resembling a pancake of Silly Putty no longer picking up images from the comics section, but now pressed into a ball for safe keeping. It rolled forward to meet the cop, stopping about ten yards from the door of the bar.

Was this what it looked like when it was dead? Small and dense like this? A cockroach after you gave it a whack, curling its legs up into itself?

If it was dead, that didn't dissuade the cop from firing. He kept his approach steady, feet at a slight angle, one in front of the other slowly, as not to trip himself up.

The bullets were no longer leaving exit wounds. The creature had consolidated all of its bones into a backstop, a thick interlocking catcher's mitt that stopped the rounds dead as they slowed in its mass, curving off after hitting the surface of its flesh like stones unsuccessfully skimmed across a muddy lake. Or at least that's what it looked like from where Vicky was standing. Maybe the curve of the bullets was an illusion, the parallax view.

After all of that, remaining still for a full minute, the desert quiet between gunshots, the thing gave a sign of life as the cop reached to his belt to reload a second time, the last of two clips from his holster. It was as if the thing had learned the pattern in one go, after absorbing thirty-one rounds, two full clips plus the one this cop must have kept in the chamber (Vicky had counted, couldn't have kicked the habit if she tried). It moved quickly, giving the cop no quarter, no chance to move.

It didn't launch itself into the air, like they had witnessed for its last two victims. No, that was cutesy showboating and this man had demonstrated that he was more than willing to use deadly force.

The shape rolled forward, taking gravel with it from where it had dug itself into the ground, expelling the crushed ballistics like it was shitting Tic Tacs, and then lashed out with an arm that formed from nothing. It was a quick motion, almost casual if Vicky was forced to anthropomorphize the blob.

The lash it formed was the dense ball of bones unfurling itself, magnetic filings dragged to the cop's polarity, to his neck. The appendage moved whip-quick, and then smoothed back into the creature again.

Only after, when the cop had begun to shoot his free hand up to his throat, when Nez's arms had once again enfolded her, yanking her off her feet and back towards the bar, did Vicky realize that the cop's arm stopped rising because his head had begun to slip from his shoulders. It twisted a bit, not like a human head would turn, but like a G.I. Joe doll, the rest of his neck, chest and shoulders remaining stock-still while the chin turned outward and began to slide.

Vicky realized what was happening, that she was being brought back inside, into protective lockup. She tried digging her heels into the dirt and wiggling against Nez's grip, but only managed to lose a shoe, a functional pump that she'd switched with her hunting boots before leaving the van this morning. She wanted to yell at Nez, to make him understand that she hadn't been kidding about the guns, that now was the time to book it to her van while the thing was occupied with the cop, *er*, ex-cop, *er*, chopped-cop, and load up on weapons.

She didn't dare speak, though. The thing was pissed off now, and it was best that they didn't give it a reason.

The mass, whatever it was, had crept over to the cop's body, arriving just as the corpse hit the dirt, legs beginning to kick softly in a hangman's twitch. The animal reached out part of itself, tentatively, before finally attaching to the man's neck stump. Gouts of blood splashed its flesh before being absorbed. The blood became bright red clouds for a moment then disappeared, fading until the color was indistinguishable from the rust brown of the rest of the shape.

Back inside the bar, the door seemed to swing closed automatically, that was until Vicky noticed Kate pressed low against it. The woman had closed the door, locked it with the key already in the deadbolt, and then tried bracing a bar stool against it, the chair toppling over each time until the woman just laid it down in front of the door.

It was a lot of proactivity for someone whose eyes were so sallow, who looked so sick from grief, even in the low light of the room. Kate's eyes were dry, though. She hadn't been crying for Ken.

The three of them went to the windows, Nez and Vicky to the one on the left, Kate taking the right for herself, now devoid of her nesting partner, her other junkie-half. Vicky felt great sadness at this: it was why you always saw them in pairs. On their own, alone and high and scared, these were just vulnerable people, real and depressing.

Vicky watched out the window, observing the now-familiar phenomenon, the feeding process, and trying to stay as detached as she could. She slipped on the same affect she used while field-stripping kill, trying to stay immune from not only the blood and guts, but the taking of a life as well.

*Know thine enemy*, or something like that. Was that the Bible or Sun Tzu? Or neither? Street Fighter, maybe? Whatever it was, she watched the horror with a critical eye, trying to spot how this thing worked.

It was growing. She'd suspected as much, but they hadn't gotten a good enough look at it when it absorbed the bartender. Now, in the twilight purple of the desert, the sky and mountainous horizon would be postcard-perfect if you cropped out all the cars and the blood. There was enough light to see by, though, she watched it add the cop's mass to its own.

That meant it would be getting stronger, heavier. Maybe heavy enough to crash the roof in over their heads if it gave it another go?

"It's getting bigger," Kate said, alone in her half of the bar-room, her whisper carrying through the stillness but still weak, sounding like the voice of a woman close to giving up.

"That's the bad news," Vicky said, feeling a smile coming on and trying her best to will it away. Self-control around other people had never been one of her strong suits, but she could do it at a card table, so why not here?

"The good news?" Nez said, not taking his eyes off of the creature, the thing almost all done with its meal now and looking spritely. There were no weeping wounds from the bullet holes, in fact, no bullet holes at all, just smooth gelatinous hide.

"I think we found a way to piss it off." Vicky said, the smile peeking through, feeling like she'd been dealt an ace and a king without even being at the table long enough to get an accurate count going. *The player has twenty-one.*

Nez and Kate both looked away from their windows now, looked to her.

Vicky was about to reveal her great secret weapon when some liquor bottles fell off the shelf, crashing down behind the bar, startling her, making Vicky realize how dark it had now gotten in here. She thought of how they'd be unable to protect themselves if somehow that thing out there wasn't alone, if there was something in here with them.

Which there was.

# Chapter Twenty-One

There was a moment when the burn seemed like it would never end, when the bullets pulled chunks of valuable mass out of his body, severing small enough parts that they could not sustain on their own, died, falling and wicking into the thirsty earth, when Felix felt fear.

It was the fear, not the man with the gun, nor his car, nor the woman sneaking around the front of the puzzle box (oh yes, he felt her too) that would be his true undoing. He'd already lost contact with the construction he left in the bar's ventilation system, the small copy of himself going dark in the white noise of panic that he'd allowed to subsume his consciousness.

But something about the attack, the reminder that even this weapon made of fire and steel could not harm him, calmed him. The burn from partially digesting the man began to fade, receding into the past as Felix allowed himself to focus on the problem in front of him, centering himself and bringing his mass under control where it had gone thin.

From there it was just a matter of the man getting close enough, then a flick of his body in one direction and the problem was solved and dinner was served.

He drank greedily, focusing on the man's torso first, the blood still flowing, still hot. Then, using his back end, he enfolded the man's head from where it had rolled, before it could cool any further and lose too many of its vital nutrients. The man's skull was large, a fine addition to Felix's collection.

As he ate, the pain of the burn now a distant memory, he felt himself grow stronger and listened to the people inside the box whisper among themselves. That's when the feeling returned to even the remotest pieces of him, a transistor radio picking up a foreign station as it bounced off the earth's curve at just the right angle.

He could feel the part of himself he'd left in the bar, then began to control its movements as it snaked through the steel vent, looking for a way out.

Felix knew what he needed to do: he needed a diversion.

# Chapter Twenty-Two

The noise came again. It was not fragments of broken bottles settling or the movement of whatever nocturnal creatures came out to Rose's after hours.

Kate had seen mouse droppings in the woman's washroom, but this was too big to be a mouse and Benny had been allergic to cats. She remembered this and marked how odd they were, the things you learned about a bartender.

There was something large and clumsy moving around behind the bar, knocking into fallen bottles, crushing shards of glass as it flailed.

The girl, Vicky, crossed the room with purpose, plucked a pool cue from off the wall and began to unscrew it, halving the stick, keeping the heavier end as a weapon and laying the other on the floor. She gave it a few swings.

"Good idea," Nez said.

"Thanks, I used to play softball in high school," Vicky said, a Texas twang in her voice now. Kate noticed that her accent was inconsistent, like she'd been trying to hide it before and had given up completely at this point. Kate of all people understood the desire to make yourself over, be different, but the body count was now sufficiently high enough that nobody cared about her bumpkin upbringing.

It wasn't quite dusk, but the sun was shifting, no longer cutting through the front windows and leaving the barroom darker now, the shadows of the tables and chairs longer.

Vicky and Nez walked to either ends of the bar, the movement coming from the center now, still clumsy, scratching against the wood frontage, probably located behind the kegs and pump system. Kate didn't think the two of them knew each other before today, but that didn't stop them from coordinating their movements nonverbally. In fact this was the only time Kate had seen the younger woman opt for a nonverbal anything.

Vicky's pink lips were sealed into a line, fixed in concentration as she brandished the pool cue, her thin arms tensed and sinewy now. Kate was witnessing a transformation, Vicky going from clown to hunter. With the height and build, never mind hairstyle, it should have been impossible to be intimidated by her, but here they were.

Reaching over the bar, peering into the darkness, Nez grabbed a half empty bottle of J&B and used the neck like a handle.

"Do you see anything?" Kate asked, but they both just shushed her.

Vicky used one of the stools to step up onto the bar and then lowered herself down the other side. Nez ducked under the hatch without lifting it. They both had their eyes narrowed to a squint. As dark as it was where Kate was standing, it must have been nearly impossible to see behind the bar.

There was no more movement as Nez and Vicky walked towards each other, just the sound of footfalls on broken glass. They were closing the distance between them, trying to trap whatever they were hearing.

"I wish I had that shoe," Vicky said. That was true, she was halfway barefoot.

Kate thought of offering her one of her own shoes, but then stopped herself from speaking, her eyes catching on something she hadn't noticed before up behind the bar. There was a section of bottles missing, displaced. Behind the hole was a small metallic square, a section of metal grating that had been misshapen, pushed out of alignment with the molding of the bar.

"Look," Kate said and pointed.

Vicky used the end of the pool cue to knock the grating to the floor where it clattered, causing Kate to jump even though she knew the sound was coming. As frightening as whatever this was, the idea that there was an internal threat to go along with the external one, at least the monster outside had stopped crashing and killing and wasn't trying to break down the walls around them. It was giving them a moment to really stew in their fear, for the sweat to dry while their hearts pounded.

Vicky moved the end of the cue to under her nose. "Yup. Smells like shit," she said.

Kate understood. Even though she hadn't stepped outside with the rest of them, she had caught a whiff of the monster through the open door, the stench of it almost moist, oppressively foul. More than just the sulfur stink of eggs or swollen garbage bags on a hot day, the smell from the creature was a symphony of rot: animal and vegetable and inorganic stenches, all mingling and pressing down on her.

"More of them?" Nez asked, backing away from the vent, back towards the hatch, fleeing the bar. Kate suddenly felt a rush of sympathy claustrophobia, even though she was standing out in the open.

It didn't seem like an act of cowardice, him wanting to escape while Vicky was still poking away back there with her cue, rolling over bottles and squinting into the darkness. Nez's retreat was tactical.

"Let's get back," he said to Vicky, echoing what Kate had already been able to tell from his body language.

"Aight," Vicky said, placing a hand flat onto the bar and vaulting upward, her ass spinning around on the lacquer, both feet crashing down onto the hardwood, her shoe leading, her bare foot coming second, unscathed from whatever sharps were coating the floor behind the bar. As extreme as her personality seemed, as improvisational and reckless, it would have taken a careful person not to cut themselves while walking through glass in the dark.

Nez didn't hop over the bar but continued his steady backwards movement out from behind it. Whatever they had heard it was keeping quiet now, the only sound Nez's breathing.

Vicky sidled up to Kate. "Hey," the girl whispered, and Kate didn't know what was coming next, a sympathetic shoulder or a jape. It seemed that Vicky was capable of anything at any moment. Instead of saying any more, the girl eased one of the straps of the Jansport off Kate's shoulder and she let it happen.

"What do you need—" she wasn't able to finish before Nez cried out.

There was more movement followed by a metallic ping that might have been the toe of Nez's boot bouncing against a nearly kicked keg.

"Fuck it's got me," Nez said, still panic in his voice but the exclamation more matter of fact than anything Kate would have been able to summon. He fell backwards and his spine hit the edge of the hatch, the length of wood straining against his weight and its own hinges, but holding. In one acrobatic move he rolled over the stretch of bar and landed on his heels, giving both Vicky and Kate a good look at the thing wrapped around his pant leg.

Nez reeled back to swing his bottle, but stopped short. He appeared to think better of it, realizing that he'd be breaking glass over his own leg.

Instead he worked the neck of the bottle down, keeping the exposed flesh of his hands away from the mass that had latched itself to him but didn't seem to be moving upward with any particular sense of urgency.

Attached to Nez's leg was a miniature version of the creature they'd just watched kill three people, one of them Ken. It didn't look particularly threatening, though. It didn't seem to breathe so there was no noise, no screeching, just the Velcro rip of its slime pulling against the tough material of Nez's jeans.

"It's biting," he said, dropping the bottle, finding little success in prying it off, the creature's skin just going thin and membranous as he pulled and then finally snapping before rejoining itself. Nez rolled towards them, into the half-light of the windows and waved them back with one hand, keeping the other fixed below his knee, kinking the muscles under his pant leg the best he could, looking like he was trying to cut off circulation, like he'd already given up on the part of the leg that the thing had touched.

Vicky was tight lipped again. With one hand she unzipped the Jansport and tore at one of the baggies, not bothering with undoing the knot or even unfixing the Ziploc. She approached Nez, shushed him the way a nurse might, and opened her balled hand, giving it a cooking-show shake.

There was another uptick of movement and Vicky jumped back. The creature was making noise now. It was sizzling, its body slackening, sounding like Pop Rocks or fresh meat on a hot stove.

The tiny bones that had given it its vaguely reptilian structure disconnected and pulled in opposite directions. This was why it hadn't eaten Ken, why it couldn't stand the touch of him: it was allergic to meth. Or something in meth, whatever the active ingredients were.

The creature detached itself from Nez's leg, hit the hardwood and began to sputter, leaving a watery slug trail as it thrashed. Vicky was smiling now.

"Have some more, fucko," she said, sprinkling another pinch on the thing, its attempt to escape backfiring as it had to spread itself thinner, provided a bigger target for Vicky to rain hellfire down on top of. Even though its bigger brother had killed Ken, Kate still felt a tightening in her throat, the feeling that she was watching unnecessary cruelty on Vicky's part, the torture of a small animal.

But the rain continued. Rocks hit jellied flesh, stuck and burned holes, the effect not unlike salt on an icy road, tiny white halos spreading as the pebbles melted.

The creature stopped moving after the third baggie had been sprinkled on top of it, even its smallest of pieces giving up their thrashing, the poisonous solution and division of its parts too much to stand. Even though the rocks were swimming in a foul, bubbling pool of ooze, the addict in Kate still spotted some crystals that looked mostly unsullied, unmelted and ingestible.

She hated herself so much.

Nez stood, rubbing his leg, opening the bottle and then smelling the lip of the glass, thinking better of it before putting his mouth to something the creature had touched.

"Any way you got like a hundred more pounds of this shit?" Vicky turned to Kate and asked.

She wished.

# Chapter Twenty-Three

The man in the sports jacket was following (okay, *and* leaving) a trail of bodies as he moved up through flyover country. He had crossed state lines three times but nothing seemed to change in regards to scenery. Even the corpses were beginning to look similar.

Some of the bodies were dead, some of them were dying and some of them would make a full recovery, their wounds superficial.

That last group the man in the sports jacket would have to kill.

The man's name? He used Steve Richardson at the hospital, where he'd introduced himself as a representative from Fish and Wildlife. Before that he'd been Dennis Ungar, intrepid reporter, who just had a few questions as to what exactly it had been that the security guard at Sam Taylor's apartment complex had seen.

The guard had been eager to talk with a reporter, especially after Dennis Ungar had told him his story would likely be a *national* headline. The guard had invited "Mr. Ungar" back to his apartment for the interview. They shared a few drinks as the guy talked about the lab 2-B project, not knowing the name for it but coming up with the term *Snotdog* which "Ungar" liked, it had a ring to it. The drinks made it easier to do what had to be done and to make it look like an accident, like after all the excitement, being interviewed by the police and the press, the guy had tied one on and forgot to breathe for just a bit too long.

Oh, his *real* name? Warren Oates. You know a Warren Oates? Whatever, it's the only name the man goes by when he's off the clock. It's more real than any of his other names because it enables him to sign his checks.

Most of the bodies he came across weren't bodies at all, more like splotches, the impression of a body, post-modernist bodies, deconstructed to really get at the heart of the matter. They indicated, to a trained eye, that there was too much blood, too many flaps of too-thin skin, for whoever had been at the epicenter of the explosion to have walked away.

The splotches weren't only human. Warren had gone off-road, hiked into the woods and saw more than a few broken tree trunks and bloody fur patches. If the Snotdog had stayed in the woods it would've made Warren's job much easier, but it hadn't and soon there would be more than mysterious power outages and abbreviated 911 calls. No, there would be iPhone footage, perfectly framed and in focus as the 'dog ran through the middle of town, picking up cars and plucking the drivers out.

If that happened, if the Snotdog made it to a densely populated area and left survivors, then someone with an equally bullshit name as Warren Oates would come looking for Warren himself. And that was an unacceptable situation.

# Chapter Twenty-Four

"*Signs?*"

"Yeah, you know. The movie. Mel Gibson is in it. It was direct-ed by the guy who did *The Sixth Sense*. Only *there* the aliens were allergic to water, which is fucking stupid because how do they breathe in our atmosphere when there's water in the air?"

"I must have missed that one," Nez said, not clear on the point Vicky was trying to make. She'd already proven fairly definitively that crystal meth could kill the monster, or at least hurt it, but what she was trying to say with the movie comparison was lost on him. That the crea-ture was an alien? It could be, but that information didn't do much for them, tactically. Maybe she was saying it just because she needed to say something, to prove to herself that she still existed. Vicky Quail was like a shark, she needed to keep swimming, keep bullshitting, or she would die.

"I remember that movie," Kate said, her voice small, reluc-tant.

"See," Vicky said, pointing over to where the woman stood, "she's ravaged her brain with hard drugs, and even she caught that one. And remembers it. No offense," Vicky said, offering not an apology but an excuse to allow herself to say whatever she wanted to, then she turned to Nez. "If she can stay apprised of the pop culture landscape, then you can too."

Kate was watching the monster out the window. They all had turned their attention outside after they'd lost interest in watching the smaller creature melt into the hardwood.

There wasn't much to see of the big one, though. The creature had been active after they'd burned its little buddy, pacing a circle around the building, slamming its bulk into the walls, seeing if it could knock its way in, but after that it had settled in to bury Ken's body and after that it just curled up on the roof of the ruined cruiser and stopped moving. It may have been sleeping, it may have been merely waiting. There was no way of knowing, and it was hard to see that far into the darkness.

It was a clear night, so at least they had the moon and the stars, but without eyes or a face of any kind, it was impossible to tell if the thing slept in the normal sense of the word.

While burying Ken, the thing had resembled a dog covering up a pile of shit. It formed strong paddle legs, breaking into the packed soil of the parking lot and forming a mound over the man's corpse. It hated the stink of him so much it didn't want to chance mistakenly touching him in whatever scuffle was yet to come. It did an okay job with his body, but left the tips of the man's sneakers exposed, the toes forming two tiny gravestones.

Burying Ken like this not only told Nez that the monster had some level of intelligence, but also that it wasn't likely to lose interest in them anytime soon: it was setting up to wait at Rose's Tavern until it got in or they came out.

"So what does that do for us? What's our next move?" Nez asked, breaking his stare out the window and turning his attention back to Vicky and the movie he'd never seen.

"Well, what happens at the end of that movie—if you take away all the insane religious subtext shit—is that everyone puts their quirks together, works as a family, and are able to defeat the aliens. It's real 'everything happens for a reason' type shit. Oh. And spoiler alert, I guess."

"You're saying everything happens for a reason?" Nez asked, finding himself wanting to speak during any pause, Vicky's pathological need to be heard becoming infectious.

"Fuck no. I'm saying that the three of us have got the tools to get out of this, if we think about it and look at what we've got."

"And what's that?"

Vicky crossed her arms, rubbing her exposed skin down, letting one tank top strap drop, the gesture part pathetic bid for warmth in the cooling bar, part striptease to stall and think. Nez was ready to offer her the shirt off his back when her expression changed, her cherry lips parting in the darkness, her individual teeth like Christmas lights.

"She and her hubby brought the meth," she said, indicating

Kate. "And I brought the guns. You…brought the handsomeness I guess, and you kept me alive, maybe. Temporarily. Which is a plus."

It was good that the room was so dark, because Nez felt a blush rise to his face despite himself. He kept the flattery out of his body language though, kept his back straight and his hand on his chin, puzzling.

"Guns?" Kate asked, seeming to be only half-listening. She wasn't watching the monster dozing on the wreck, her eyes were lower than that, fixed on something else out the window. Then Nez realized she was watching the mound where her man lay. It was like she was expecting him to get back up, his neck to uncollapse itself and his head to pop back out of his chest cavity.

"I've never tried it myself, but I've heard of roughnecks filling shotgun shells with rock salt or black eyed peas. For when they didn't want to kill someone, just send their kneecaps a message. I've got boxes of shells in my van. If I get out there, replace some birdshot with some of that crystal blue persuasion she's got, I bet the charge wouldn't vaporize the rocks completely, I bet I could blast that mofo apart."

It sounded too theatrical, like something that could work without a hitch in the movies, but wouldn't hold water in real life. Her plan was the chassis of Steve McQueen's Mustang repairing itself between cuts, the hubcaps reaffixing themselves after flying off in all directions, unbeholden to the laws of physics. But her excitement wasn't only palpable, it was unstoppable. Even if it were sure to kill her, Vicky would be trying her plan with or without his consent. Now all Nez had to do was think of a scenario in which the attempt didn't get them all killed.

"Then we ride off into the night?"

"Yeah, is your truck fast?"

"Probably faster than your bus."

"Watch it," Vicky said, no longer shivering, either reinvigorated by the plan, warmed by her own ingenuity, or never cold in the first place, rubbing herself down just part of the show.

Nez tried to think of how they could achieve this, whether he was going to let Vicky run to her van alone, as far as it was from the front door of the bar, but Kate beat him to it.

"You're going to need a diversion," the woman said, eyes still fixed out the window, listening more closely than he had suspected. She was right.

# Chapter Twenty-Five

Vicky Quail talked everywhere, to everyone, but she did not talk at the movies.

It was one of the few clauses in the social contract to which she strictly adhered.

Like hunting, the movies provided hours of Zen calm. Also like hunting, she had picked up her affinity for movies from her father.

She only killed what she could eat, or, if she needed the money, what she was sure she could sell for a profit. The rest of her income came from the tables, not that she needed much income. For Vicky, the occasional tattoo was a luxury, and a bit more regularly she would spring for a bottle of nail polish. Besides ammunition, gas and the rent on her tiny apartment, she had no other expenses but movie tickets.

Messy as it was, dinky as it was, her father's apartment had been the greatest place in the world. Stacks of books and magazines and poster tubes: a lifetime worth of memorabilia that had at one time, barely in Vicky's memory, been spread across several rooms of the house her parents had shared in together, before the divorce.

In his small apartment, the paraphernalia was concentrated, too cramped to be a proper display, no longer a collection but a mausoleum. Once he'd moved out there was no room for file cabinets to hold the lobby cards, no attic to house boxes of newspaper clippings.

She'd get dropped off at his place after school on every third Friday, sometimes her mom reeking of pot, booze, or worse. Vicky risked taking the ride with her mom because she wanted, needed, to see her father.

Vicky needed to sit next to him at dollar matinees, and then they'd do their best to sneak into any other theater, or if it was a single screen, stay to watch the film again. At home, her father would spend the day explaining the vast history of the movies to her, recounting third- and fourth-hand stories about studio-era Hollywood stars, people she'd never seen outside the photographs in his house, the low-quality telecined VHS tapes he had stacked under his modest tube TV.

The only spot of the apartment that wasn't crowded with fire hazards was the hall closet, a shrine to her father's *other* hobby, hunting. Both the rifle and shotgun were kept unloaded, gun locks around their triggers. This was not a habit that Vicky kept into adulthood, but then again she didn't have any kids. Hunting and movies were the two sides of her father's personality, order and discord, cleanliness and mess. It was a schism that he'd passed on, either through hereditary or upbringing.

If she tried to think about those times without a sheen of nostalgia, remembered in her middle school days when she had a growing self-awareness, the times she'd begun to suspect that her father was an obsessive and a loser, she would hurt inside.

If she hurt, she would invariably think of the Friday she was picked up from school and *didn't* go to her father's place.

He'd died on a Monday and it had taken until the Friday, when Vicky asked why they weren't going to his apartment complex, for her mother to work up the nerve to tell her.

Her mother had pulled to the side of the road, tried her best to look sorry, and said, "His landlord called me, honey. Your dad passed away."

There was melodrama after that, in her mother's car. Not clean Hollywood melodrama, tossed drinks and witty putdowns from spurned lovers, no it was more Lifetime movie than that: unadulterated sap. Not a movie her dad would have watched.

Vicky ducked and rolled out of the moving car as her mother tried to keep driving in the opposite direction, back towards their house that still felt empty even though her dad's stuff had been moved out years ago.

Then she ran, taking alleys and backyards until she was sure she'd lost her mother, then arrived at his apartment. On that run, she hated Vegas, wished for the early days when her parents had been together and they'd had the wide-open spaces of West Texas, not the clutter of a city.

She'd sobbed the whole run, her voice cracking as she sucked in air. Puberty was setting in, but she was still more little girl than anything else, she didn't know then that she would only gain another three inches, tops, of height before she was finished growing.

Her mother had to have known where Vicky was heading, so it was either negligence or compassion for her daughter's emotional state that caused her to delay. Vicky liked to choose sympathy, the idea that her mother was purposefully giving her space to process her father's death, but it was just as likely that her mom had stopped off at 7-11 for cigarettes before picking her distraught offspring up at her dead ex-husband's apartment.

The locks hadn't been changed, so Vicky was able to use her key to get inside, but when she did she found bare walls, stretches of hardwood flooring that she hadn't even known were there because she was so used to takeout boxes and old *TV Guide*s.

Her father's belongings were gone. The only things he valued, the things besides Vicky, were missing. It wasn't possible, nothing had been brought to their house.

Then Vicky had a grotesque thought, one that propelled her down three flights of stairs, nearly end over end if she hadn't been just with it enough to grab the banister, almost tugging it out of the sheetrock.

Behind the apartment building, one of Vegas' oldest, three floors of calcified bathroom drains and shitty climate control, she found what she'd feared she would: a full dumpster.

It stank as she approached and she tried to guess when the garbage pickup was scheduled for this street. Ten minutes away, in Vicky's neighborhood, garbage day was Thursday, but it must have been different here: this dumpster was both full and rank.

Standing at the bottom of the structure, sure that the smell would only get worse as she peeked over the edge, she pinched her nose with one hand and reached to one rung with the other. The metal was scalding, even though the dumpster was in shadow now. It must have spent all day in the sun, the contents baking, the sides becoming superheated.

Vicky did not recoil from the heat. Instead she soaked up the pain and used it to spurn her climb upwards, used it as fuel to push her forward, the rubber of her sneakers going spongy as she clambered against the side, her toes slipping.

The lip of the dumpster was thick enough for her to kneel without touching garbage, the fabric of her shorts just long enough to cover her knees.

She perched and looked, and eventually, once she took in the spoiled Chinese food soaking into her father's books on Billy Wilder, the curdled milk pooling between the covers of his press kits from the sixties and seventies, she cried some more, even harder than she had on the way over here. Vicky cried not just for herself, but for her father, what he would have felt seeing a lifetime of collecting end up like this. As if the indignities of uprooting his collection to a flophouse apartment wasn't enough, it had to be thrown out with the garbage.

There was the sound of tires on gravel in the alleyway behind her, but she didn't look towards it.

Her mother had shown up, finally.

Now with an audience, Vicky felt a desire to jump down into the garbage, to her father's collection, to make a show of throwing herself on the casket. Maybe she would scratch herself on some scrap metal hiding underneath the paper goods and need a tetanus shot. That would teach her.

At the last moment she stopped herself, told herself that such a display would have been self-serving, not really about her father, just angsty teen shit.

"I've got his guns in the garage back home, along with a few boxes of things. It couldn't all stay, Vicky."

It was the most compassionate sentence she could ever remember her mother saying to her and it would be forever linked with a strong sense memory: the stink of rotting garbage.

♦

That was partly what the thing had smelled like, and that was probably why Vicky was getting the vapors now as she tried to stuff napkins down the neck of a bottle of rum.

The paper was getting too soggy and slipping too far down to be easily lit. Her desire to cry and curl up into a ball was either the memory of her father's ruined collection, frustration at the bottle, or she was closer than she thought to her period. If she was told that the monster had incubated in that dumpster, she would have believed it.

"This will work?" Nez asked, Vicky hearing two separate questions: *Will this light?* And *Am I going to light myself on fire?* She looked down at the Molotov-in-progress.

"As long as this bottle's not three parts water, yeah, it should light."

"Benny wouldn't do that, he was a good bartender," Kate said.

"Sure he wouldn't." Vicky baffled herself with the tone of that one, not knowing whether she was being conciliatory or sarcastic.

Nez lifted up a rag from under the bar and Vicky started to snake it into the bottle, finding much more success than she had with the napkins. She kept talking to make it sound like she knew what she was doing.

"That thing that I pried off the top was a flame catch. It comes on the bottle and it wasn't put there by Benny. It's in place to keep frat boys from turning their Hawaiian shirt parties into full-pig luaus. This stuff will light. Believe it."

Vicky handed him the bottle and then tore a match out of the book she'd placed on the bar. Nez took a step back, keeping the bottle at arm's length, the wick dripping onto his hands.

"I'm not gonna light you now. Jesus." She pinched the match between the striker and the cover and pulled. The match lit, adding a tiny light to the darkness of the barroom. She didn't know why she was testing them, matches didn't go bad. Maybe she was stalling, maybe she wanted to smell the smoke to forget the stink of garbage.

"Aight," she said, jumping down off the bar stool, then reaching into her front pocket, taking out her key ring and replacing it with two baggies of meth, stuffing another two in one of her back pockets. That should be enough. Taking the whole backpack would have been dumb; it wasn't even mentioned in the scenario they discussed, her taking the entirety of their secret weapon stockpile with her on her possible suicide mission was a no go.

The only point of contention was whether she stayed in the van to load up or tried to grab enough supplies and run back inside the bar with them.

It was agreed upon that she would "play it by ear" but that wasn't what she was going to do. It would be a waste of time (and possibly ammunition) if she tried to get back to the bar, never mind the most likely way to get crushed into Vicky pâté as the monster ran back to the front, realizing that it had been tricked.

"When you throw it, make sure it arcs high enough to break, but don't coat yourself with a hundred and eighty proof liquor. I'd say underhand, but you do whatever you feel comfortable with," Vicky said, the coach offering last-minute pointers.

Nez looked at her, wiping his hands on his jeans but not breaking his deadpan eye contact. Between them the smoke curled up from the extinguished match, a tiny orange speck still hanging on in the darkness. "I'm not comfortable with any of this," Nez said.

"Don't be such a puss," she said to him before turning to Kate. "And you know what you're doing, Smokey?"

"Um, screaming?" Kate said, not confident in the answer, still in a fog that was either grief or drug related. *It's probably time for baby to have her bottle*, Vicky thought.

"Yup, perfect. When I'm out there, keep being noisy in here, try to make up for my absence," she said, both a self-aware joke and a direct order. They had no idea how smart the thing was, how it was able to see and hear, or if those were even applicable terms. "Good luck," she added, letting the two of them know that the mission was on, that they needed to be ready.

Vicky began to back towards the front of the room, Kate and Nez moving to the back door like they were supposed to.

"Just like this?" Kate asked.

"Just like this. You guys get back there, when our big buddy is off the car and around the building, I'll make my run for it. I'll try not to slam the door, so when you see the fucker, close the door, even if you're not sure I'm out yet."

No risks, everyone does their part and no more.

"And then we wait," Nez said, a resignation in his voice, a displeasure that he would have so little control of things once she was out the door and would not be able to enfold Vicky in his arms, wrestling her back to safety.

Yeah, she would miss that too.

# Chapter Twenty-Six

"Come and get it, you asshole!"

Felix did not understand these words. He could barely distinguish between the male and female voices buffeting the hills and ricocheting back towards the road.

"Hey. We're talking to you. Come on!" After that there were more sounds, prolonged shouts that did not have the peculiar peaks and valleys of language.

All Felix really understood was that the food was out of the box, or at least had uncovered enough of an opening to allow itself to be heard. All Felix needed was a window, opened maybe two foot by one, and then he'd be able to squeeze himself inside.

He wanted to move with haste, but his body had loosened, sunken against the hood of the wrecked car, his flesh sinking into the cracks, the divide between the hood and the engine block, enfolding the tubing and wires, cementing himself. He willed his bones to stand, sucking his flesh free of every porous surface he'd allowed it to set into.

They were so loud, the waves of their voices were so prevalent that Felix could feel the vibrations in his flesh, even as he formed four legs and began to pump, the suspension of the wrecked cruiser propelling him upward as he shifted the bulk of his weight into the air.

He could not hear footsteps, though, which meant that they either weren't outside at all or were very close to shelter. He would have to be quick, quick enough to round the corner of the box (he'd already tried leaping over it, they'd be expecting that) and take them before they could barricade themselves again.

Felix did not know the term for frustration, for bloodlust, but they were certainly feelings with which he was intimately acquainted.

# Chapter Twenty-Seven

Vicky watched as the creature—with far less speed than it had moved in the daylight—rose from the top of the police cruiser and padded onto the packed dirt road, the nose of the vehicle bobbing like a diving board.

It stayed low to the ground, the bones inside of it shifting and reconfiguring so that as it pushed forward its form shrank and spread. After a moment its highest point stayed no more than three feet of the ground, a giant wriggling flatworm, stalking its prey.

From the back of the building, Nez and Kate continued yelling. Kate swore like a dockworker, something that seemed out of character for the mousey woman. But then again, Vicky reminded herself that she didn't much know what the woman was capable of or how much Ken's death had affected her. It's not that Vicky didn't care, or that she hadn't warmed to Kate, they simply didn't have time.

Outside the window, the creature's movement accelerated. There was still stealth to it, but not anything that worried Vicky. Nez and Kate would see the monster coming, it was a large shadow moving across the desert, even though its flesh and bone were undulating like tank treads and she couldn't hear it from inside.

It had to be making some kind of noise. Nez would keep his situational awareness, was competent. He used to be a cop, right?

*No. Focus!* She chastised herself for the jitters, for fixating on a part of the plan that was completely outside of her control. Besides, Nez and the junkette got to run back inside when they were finished, and her assignment was much more dangerous.

She looked at her van, the shape of the creature rounding the corner of the building now, ducking out of sight. It was thirty seconds to show time, she estimated, and began to count.

*30.* She moved into position behind the door.

*29.* If she entered the van through the side door she would make more noise. *27.* But would be closer to her weapons and ammo. *25.* No, the passenger's side door was her best option, she could unlock it, get inside and dive back into the cab without much noise. *23.*

She took the large round key between two fingers and dug into her palm with the teeth. *20.* With her other hand she gripped the door handle, double-checked that the deadbolt wasn't thrown. *17.* Nez and Kate stopped what they were yelling midsentence, and Kate began screaming.

*15.* There was a faux dawn, a new sun rising from behind the bar, the shadows in the parking lot reappearing and then going long as the fireball rose up into the night. Then there was an explosion that rattled the building, shook the doorpull in Vicky's hand.

*Fuck it.*

She pulled back and felt the cool night air replace the beer-lacquered oak smell of the bar. But only for a moment, because as she stepped outside she felt the heat of the fireball press down upon her from where it had risen over the bar.

With one hand she scooped up her lost shoe and had it over her toes, hopping into the heel without losing much momentum.

Instead of running straight and then turning to hit the side of the van, she ran in a soft arc, the curve calling for less accuracy and expending less effort.

As her arms pumped, instead of focusing on her task as she ran she couldn't help but wonder what had caused the explosion. They knew there may have been some kind of accelerant out in the shed, propane or gasoline or both, but there was also the possibility that Nez hadn't thrown the bottle far enough and had instead torched Benny's car. If that happened, would the blaze be too close, would the bar catch fire?

Her feet were out of her control, bringing her to meet the side of the van too fast. She put her hands out and skidded, hitting the door and bouncing but not losing her footing.

She unclenched her hand from around the key. Her fingers had gone white, speckled with red where the teeth had dug in, but still she was able to drive the end of the key home with one plunge. Vicky pressed and turned, the tiny grind of the tumblers like the trumpets of angels. The door pulled open with only a slight creak, nothing that could probably be heard from the other side of the building, especially over the roar of the fire. The blaze was still high enough that looking behind her she could see the corona outlining Rose's Tavern, lighting the desert around her.

Maybe the blast had been spotted from the highway, perhaps there would be fire crews here soon. Not that that inspired much confidence. It had been over two hours and still nobody had come to check on the dead cop.

Diving inside, she scattered the remains of yesterday's Carl's Jr. lunch/dinner with her knees. *Wow, that wasn't that long ago*, she thought. It also explained why she was so hungry, that was her last meal. She could dig around for protein bars, she may even still have some field rations tucked under the seat, but first she had a job to do.

She had two tackle boxes in the back of the van. One was filled with tackle, the other she had stripped of two of its drawers and used it to store her ammo. She had hunting licenses, but sometimes it was just easier to slip her rifle into a rod tube and look like she was entering a park to fish.

The initial fireball had lit up the outside world like daytime, but now that the flames had diminished there was just a dim beam of light entering into the van through the treated back windows. The light was enough to see shapes, the outline of things, but Vicky would have preferred to have more to work by.

She had two boxes of shells, buckshot and birdshot. Twelve shells in each. The lighter charge and smaller pellets of the birdshot would be less likely to pulverize the meth crystals, but the buckshot would make a bigger hole.

She decided to mix them up, alternate so she had some of each.

With the shells in a pile between her thighs, she sat cross-legged and laid both baggies in front of her, using the top of the tackle box as an improvised workbench.

It was tempting, so tempting, to switch on one of her electric lanterns, but she stopped herself. Kate's screaming had ceased as soon as the blast had started. Had the flames, meant as both a signal flare and a distraction, engulfed the monster, burnt it up? Could Nez be knocking on the window to the van at any moment with a change in plans, their escape ensured, the creature vanquished without her there to witness it?

It was possible, but unlikely. The monster didn't seem stupid enough to walk into the flames, and it had already proven itself adept at stop-drop-and-roll after it had mistakenly gotten a taste of Ken's body.

*Does the silence mean they're both dead?* It was an even worse line of questioning and she pushed it away.

Her fingers worked fast in the darkness, undoing the crimping at the mouth of the shells, emptying out the bearings, halving the portions, some of the metal sticking to her sweaty palms, and then mixing the remainder with the grey crystals, replacing them into the tube, packing them onto the primer with her thumb and recrimping the top.

The process was not unlike rolling coins, in the days before she could go to the supermarket, use that counting machine they had and then take her money in Bass Pro Shops gift cards in order to waive the usage fee. She had three shells finished, two birdshot and one buck before she realized that there was a meditative quality to the act. Filling the shells helped lower her heart rate, the hammering of blood in her ears dissipating, allowing her to hear what was going on outside.

It allowed her to hear the thudding, the footsteps on gravel that were too loud to be human, that were coming right towards her.

Vicky Quail panicked and threw her hands up to the gun rack, taking down the twelve gauge break-action, her father's gun, and pulling it to her just in time for the world around her to spin. Her body went airborne, the force that had hit the van so great that the van didn't just flip onto its side, but was sent spinning.

As if in slow motion, she could see the prepared shells whisk off the top of the tackle box, float in zero g for a moment before everything crashed to a halt, herself included.

# Chapter Twenty-Eight

Police scanners were a dime a dozen, you could probably find at least two in every frat house in America, but the man named Warren Oates had access to something a little better (and a shitload more illegal) than a police scanner.

The initial call from dispatch to the highway patrol unit hadn't aroused much suspicion, single vehicle car crashes happened all the time. Even if it seemed difficult to crash in the desert, with nothing to collide with and no one else around, the incident was just one of many leads Warren was keeping an ear out for as he drove.

An hour and a half later, when dispatch called the guy they'd sent out back to check on his progress, and the guy hadn't responded, *that* was when Warren figured it worth investigating. He pulled to the side of the road and typed the name of the bar into the laptop he had resting on the passenger's seat, the machine through which he was running the extra-legal program that allowed him to respond on the highway patrol band.

"Dispatch, this is…" He paused as he read a piece of information from a smaller window on his desktop, a list of active cars in the area. "Laughlin, four nine two two. I couldn't help but hear what you've got going on. I'm not far from there and can check on your trooper and radio you back when I find him. Over."

The female dispatcher said, "One moment two-two," then paused. She was looking for him in their computer. She'd be able to see his car, she most likely had the same list as Warren, but she wouldn't be able to see the real four nine two two's GPS location as he highly doubted that the departments shared that information.

"Thank you two-two, I'll be waiting to hear back from you. Much obliged, over," she said, Warren thinking that if this dispatcher or car four nine two two ever got back in touch with each other, it may be over dinner and a movie.

"No problem, dispatch, happy to help," Warren said, the smile in his voice not a lie. He was more than happy to help track down her missing cop.

He would have to backtrack, then loop around, but the two-hour trip the Garmin was estimating could be cut down if he stepped on it.

The man who went by Warren Oates took the next turn-off and opened the car up into the cool desert night, the sound of liquid sloshing in his trunk as he accelerated.

# Chapter Twenty-Nine

It was hard to imagine any part of the plan going better.

Nez hadn't been the one to spot the creature as it inched towards them, flattening itself against the building and crawling across the outer wall like a slug.

"There," Kate yelled and pointed. The creature was less than fifteen feet from them, but stretched so thin it was nearly invisible unless you knew that the wall wasn't normally spackled with human mandible and tibia bones.

Nez planted the ass end of the bottle between his knees, angling the rag away from his crotch but trying not to spill high-proof liquor onto his boots.

"Get in," he said and Kate complied, stepping back into the doorway as he struck the match, the heavy door propped open by his back.

The flame bloomed atop the bottle before he could even touch the match to the rag, the vapors of the rum enough to ignite it. He was surprised at the sound it made, a whooshing hiss that he was certain meant the bottle was about to explode, shooting hot glass into his belly and dick.

The substance clinging to the wall hadn't moved when they'd looked, pointed and talked at it, but it sure hustled when Nez lit the Molotov.

Tendrils sucked themselves free of the aging siding, not reaching for Nez, but drawn like liquid metal to the magnet of the hissing flame.

Nez reeled back and tossed, ignoring the blue flame that engulfed his hand, burning too briefly to do any damage before the spilt alcohol was gone. His knuckles would be silky smooth, maybe even a little red, but he'd be fine.

There was a moment he was worried the creature would be too quick, would catch the bottle midair as it launched itself off the building towards the shed, stopping the bomb from exploding. The thing was fast but it wasn't that fast. The bottle hit the pile of debris, the former shack, dead center and the flame spread out over the splintered wood and twisted metal.

The creature jumped to the top of Benny the bartender's car, the weight of it busting out the windows as Nez moved back into the doorway, the door partially closing behind him but not enough that he wasn't taken off his feet by the second blast.

Either the generator had been full-to-bursting with fuel or there was a propane tank in the wreckage. Whatever the case, the explosion was huge, the gust of air so hot that it singed the hair of his nostrils.

The back door blew closed and above him Kate threw the locks, keeping her cool in a way that he wasn't sure he'd be able to. Before he stood, his first instinct was to have her stop, open the door so they could see if the creature had been destroyed in the blast, but that was a dangerous instinct, one that ran contrary to their plan. The persistence of gut feelings like that was the reason Nez didn't trust himself around guns anymore.

Pressing themselves against the door, Nez and Kate listened, warm air whistling through the crack below them, rising and making it uncomfortably hot in the back room of Rose's Tavern. He could hear the roar of flames, already diminishing, not much out there to burn.

"Do you hear it?" Nez asked, not sure if the blast had deafened him. The roaring sound he was hearing might have been the white noise of his own burst eardrums.

Before Kate could speak, the door rattled against its hinges from a blow so savage Nez was sure they'd be crushed under it by a second knock.

Kate grabbed him by the shoulders and pulled him away. It was the second time that she'd shown more savvy, had done a better job of protecting them than he could protecting all of them.

The beast was still alive, but was it swathed in flames? Was it spreading the fire to the wall and roof, ready to smoke them out? Had all this been a mistake? Were they going to burn alive? Was the monster going to have a hot meal?

As if in answer, the door shook again. Standing back from the frame, it was easier to see that the creature proved a real threat. If it kept at it, it would break the door down.

There was a third hit, not at the door this time, but the wall, rattling cleaning supplies off the shelf to the right. The animal didn't even realize that its best bet was a continued battery against the door.

They may not have killed it, but they were safe for the moment.

Both of them stood tense, waiting, but there was no fourth hit. The creature had either died or retreated or…

"Let's get back up to the bar," Nez said, pushing Kate in front of him, the small passageway not wide enough for both of them abreast.

There was another thump against the side of the building, this time to their left, the beams shaking above their heads, dust falling from somewhere. The thing was headed back to the parking lot, same as them, but it was testing the walls of the building on the way there.

They were supposed to get its attention, rile it up, but they may have done too good a job. Perhaps the creature's vision wasn't heat-based, perhaps it just liked the heat, maybe it got energy from it. Like how Superman's strength came from the sun. Nez thought about his pop culture knowledge, how Vicky had questioned the integrity of it mere minutes before, and thought that: hey, at least he had that one.

*Please don't let it get her*, he found himself pleading with nobody in particular.

Reaching the back of the bar, Nez vaulted over the counter, his leg catching on one of the taps but the pull breaking free instead of yanking him back. It clattered to the floor, wood splintering under his boots.

He heard the initial hit before he reached the window to see the van twirling in the air, making a complete twist before landing on its roof, rocking to a halt, the windows cracking but all the ones he could see remaining miraculously intact.

Vicky hadn't given it a reason to attack her, to know that she was there. She hadn't shot a gun, hadn't yelled and screamed like they had, but still it had known. This meant that it wasn't as deaf or as stupid as they'd hoped.

David Nez noted this, but the new information didn't seem like it meant a goddamn thing as the creature began to wrap itself around the van and squeeze.

There would be no more fighting this monster, it was going to win.

# Chapter Thirty

Vicky wasn't knocked unconscious, just knocked senseless, knocked broken, faring about as well as a porcelain doll would when faced with the spin cycle.

The corner of one tackle box had caught her just under her right eye, leaving not only a bruise so bad the hit may have fractured her orbital, but a deep cut on the thin skin there.

The blood flowed immediately and profusely.

At least the box hadn't opened and showered her with fish hooks while everything spun, bounced against the walls. *It's all about the little victories*, she thought.

This fucking thing had dropped a tree on her earlier today and it still wasn't contented, had to try to one-up itself. She flicked the safety off on the shotgun. She'd managed to keep a hold of the weapon, and holding tight had given her something to do with her arms and hands as her legs pin-wheeled.

Looking around, she considered switching the break-action for a more modern weapon, but there was no time. Besides, this was now her lucky gun.

She cracked opened the chamber and began to scan the wreckage around her for the shells. It was easier said than done. The three finished shells had become mixed up with the regular pile, all of them scattered along the van like balls in a keno bubble, most of them resting on the ceiling, now the floor.

She watched blood drip from her eye, predominately with her left, the vision going in and out of watery in the right, battered one. The blood dripped onto old fast food bags and junk mail, a handwritten list of all the casinos she'd been barred from, partly to remind her where not to visit, partly to keep count for bragging rights. Thankfully the blood also dripped onto the ammunition, highlighting it.

Vicky's hands were wonky, wouldn't obey. She felt drunk, trying to control her arms and fingers like she was a marionette with limited points of articulation, body separate from brain. She willed her fingers to close around a green and copper shell, the color of birdshot, lifted it to her left eye and peered down into the cylinder. It was not one of the special shells: there were no gems of methamphetamine mixed with the pellets.

She tossed it behind her and as she tried again, the van began to shift beneath her. It was not her head injury, she was actually moving. The roof of the van scraped across the packed earth of the parking lot. The creature must have been pushing her along, the curved steel of the roof leaving a trail in the dirt. Whether she was moving towards the bar or away from it she couldn't tell, she was a little turned around.

*I need to ignore it,* she told herself, knowing that once it figured out that it could just push through the cracked glass of the back windows, it would be upon her.

There was an ache under her weight. The pain was where her spine met her ass and she sent her hand to investigate. She came back with two shells, one of them bearing the tampered-with top and crystal glisten of her secret weapon.

Above her the van groaned, started to rock side to side. The creature was on top of her and she imagined big feet crushing her muffler flat, a maw of sharpened bones tearing at her tires.

She pushed them into the break and pressed both shells flat, strained to hinge the two halves of the weapon back into firing position, the stock slipping out from under her arm, the wood slick with her face-blood Two or three of her fingers were broken, her thumb and her pointer doing most of the work, flicking the end up.

There were sounds on all sides of her now, the light filtering in the back windows going dimmer. Instead of attacking the guts of the van, the creature was stretching itself around the vehicle, surrounding her.

Pain shot up Vicky's legs as she tried to move, each of her knees feeling like they were in a billion jagged pieces. She pressed her spine up against one of the seats and faced the back window. Wedging the back of the shotgun between the headrest and the remainder of the upside-down driver's seat, she used the leverage to arm the weapon, pulling back the hammers.

There was silence, the goo on the other side of the back windows not looking like it was doing much to break in, flecks of bone and grit floating inside it, looking like a fish tank filled with dirty chewing gum.

That's when the walls and ceiling began to close in around her, the van getting smaller around the middle, the seat she'd been leaning up against beginning to pinch her ass hard as the headrest dug into the ceiling.

The back windows burst inward, but instead of covering Vicky with glass, most of the shards stuck in place, attached to the creature as it ebbed inward. The wave of slime fell in towards her but did not resolve itself into a lash like the creature had used to kill the cop.

Maybe it didn't see her.

Instead of instant ignoble death, the van continued to collapse around her, the center, where the chassis and walls offered the least resistance, becoming the middle of a crushed Coke can, the floor, ceiling and sides of the van ready to meet in seconds. Vicky pulled her legs towards her, the pain in them immense, but she needed to curl them in to avoid amputation.

Somewhere in the shifting and movement, one of her lanterns had been twisted on, the unnaturally bright light making her blood look cartoonish.

The creature was closing her off from itself, at least from the back window of the van, the walls collapsing like the aperture of a camera. Vicky turned, quarters getting increasingly tight as the roof sloped, rising up under her. She imagined what it had to have looked like from outside the van, the vehicle being constricted by a giant predatory snail. It would be comical if she wasn't about to be brutally murdered.

With a view from between the two front seats, a half-foot-wide window that she was able to stick the barrel of the shotgun through, she watched the windshield spider web, withstanding more punishment than she thought it could, but still doomed to fail, and soon.

Turned forward now, peering out the windshield through the semi-translucent yellow-green goo of the creature's flesh, Vicky could see the outline of Rose's Tavern.

She prayed that she wouldn't see the door open, wouldn't have to watch the other two get themselves killed in a vain attempt to save her, but the door held firm, like they'd planned. She didn't know whether to be relieved or let down that Nez was keeping his word, wasn't coming to wrap those big arms around her.

In the middle of the windshield, a skull floated, half of the teeth missing, still flecked with enough flesh that she guessed it had belonged to the cop, in life. His dead eyes watched her, white and red, the pupils and eyelids eroded away so the globes were just specks in the blackness. Then the skeletal nose began to knock against the glass, weakly at first, but with a persistence that became a banging. There was more squeezing, more constricting focusing on the front half of the van, she was thankful she was small, that she wouldn't be immediately crushed to death and would get one chance to do some damage before it was upon her.

The windshield cracked some more. This was it. Vicky put her finger on the trigger, made sure the blast was angled at the middle of the window, center mass.

In front of her, the windshield shattered, but instead of merely falling in, the wave of the creature pushed towards her, a liquid filling all the available space in a container.

She sucked in a breath of air, her last before the creature was touching her, and fired.

The jellied flesh of the creature was pushed back by the blast, speckled with dark spots, but it didn't go nuts like it had when it had touched Ken.

That had been the normal shell.

Before she could fire again the creature was wrapping around her arms and hands, its flesh feeling hotter than she expected it to, like jumping into an unclean Jacuzzi at the rattiest hotel on the strip.

There underwater, she was swallowed up, the pain in her arm starting as the beast began to wrench her apart. The smell was in her nose, even though she hadn't breathed in. The thing had pushed itself up into her nostrils.

*God, just let it be quick,* she thought and Vicky Quail fired one more shot.

# Chapter Thirty-One

Kate found the whole ordeal difficult to watch, not because there was blood and guts to see, but because there wasn't.

Watching the creature's attack on the van was similar to an apartment fire as seen from the street, knowing that people were burning alive inside, but the horrors of your imagination were maybe even worse than witnessing the real thing.

When the van had somersaulted—the contents inside it possibly stuck to the sides by centrifugal forces, but probably not—there was a chance that Vicky was dead. When the center of the van had been crushed, there was a chance that Vicky was dead.

She hadn't been dead, though, not any of those times. It had taken a few tense moments between each onslaught for signs of life, but they had come. There were glimmers of movement, visible by the glow of synthetic lantern light from inside the van. As the creature wrapped itself around the vehicle, encompassing the windows, popping the latches on the door with its strength, it was lit by the lantern, the effect of putting your hand over a flashlight's bulb, watching your skin go orange and red, getting to see the outline of your finger's bones.

Then the creature dove inside the windshield, its body moving so fast it punctured one of the tires as it scrambled to get its entire self inside, the sound and wind from the blowout frightening the monster and displacing some of its mass.

Then the creature was met with some resistance.

The first blast was muffled, more a flash of light and a distant thunder-crack than it was a gunshot, but the second shot caused a violent reaction that had reminded Kate of mixing Mentos and Diet Coke.

The creature split down the middle, an exit wound not caused by the blast itself but by the creature pulling itself apart trying to get away from whatever it had just been peppered with.

It had no mouth, no lungs that weren't liquefied, so it didn't scream. There was something odd about that, watching the thrashing, the movements of an animal in pain, but the animal remaining completely mute.

Back when Kate had been in recovery, while she was pregnant with Dale, when things had been good with Tommy, the two of them had decided that they needed more culture in their lives and had attended the ballet.

It was a small troupe, there wasn't much high art in Vegas, but that didn't matter. Kate and Tommy couldn't tell the difference between three- and thirty-dollar wine, so they weren't going to know good ballet from bad.

Going to the recital was a step, though, a step towards the comfortable middle-class life that had seemed so possible back then, when Dale was alive, safe. They were inoculating Kate against a relapse with culture, drowning out the memory of the bad days with music therapy.

She'd tried not to think it during the show, tried to engage the art, but there was something so silly about the dancers, their expressions and bodies reaching the height of different emotions, but never once speaking. She wanted to slap the premier, get him just to talk to the girl he loved, tell her how she felt.

That was the creature: twirling, almost ripping itself in two during its death dance, but the only sound was the whipping and fall of sand across the parking lot, the small tinkle of safety glass dripping from the van's frame.

It had moved so fast, had folded in upon itself, becoming phallic then vaginal then back again, undulating like a plastic bag underwater, that Kate hadn't taken conscious notice of what had made its movements so human. She didn't see it until Nez gasped beside her, his expression an intangible pre-grief, the look of exhilaration turning to horror.

It looked so small in the mass of the thing, getting close enough to the window, backlit by the lighted van, that Kate could see how all the fingers had curled except for one, like it was pointing.

Inside the dancing beast, its movements slowing, was the tiny, tattooed arm of Vicky Quail, that little girl who had tried to be so mean to Kate when they'd first met, but had shown more courage than any of them could have mustered.

# Chapter Thirty-Two

Nez didn't have a problem with gore. He'd seen his share, could handle it in real life about as well as he could in viewing crime scene photos he sought out on the internet, when he was playing arm-chair detective.

As Navajo Nation, it seemed like half his time had been spent responding to calls about kids blowing their fingers off with M-80s. Those were quarter sticks of dynamite that were sold as fireworks, but served up no entertainment beyond a loud bang and the chance that you might get to see your buddy lose a digit. Maybe the time spent on that was an exaggeration, but it had happened at least twice, every time Nez arriving before the paramedics.

Since quitting, staring at mutilation had become one of his few hobbies, not in a morbid way, but in a clinical one.

The arm was nothing like any of that. It was somehow worse and less believable.

For Nez, bodily destruction on any scale beyond a few dime-sized bullet holes or a missing pinky took on the sheen of unreality, even when he was staring at it, knew it to be true. As Vicky's arm floated there, pointing to the sky, then to the ground, like it was trying to tell them something, and then just spinning like a top as the creature tried to rub itself clean in the dirt, the arm could have been a latex special effect.

The skin didn't look right, it was waxen and pale. The gnarled end of the wound, pulled out like spun sugar, not severed cleanly like the cop's head had been, looked too dark, even in the starlit gloom of the parking lot, the fluorescent glow of the destroyed van hitting it from the side, it seemed like it should have been redder, if it were *real*.

"What do we do?" Kate said, breaking the spell, allowing Nez to avert his eyes from Vicky's dismemberment.

It was a good question. Not only did they not have a plan B: their plan A had no subsections, no footnotes as to what should happen if it was quasi-successful.

The creature's movements slowed, and there was a space of time where it looked like it was deflating, was a moment away from losing all control over its form and dying, to be absorbed back into the sand and shrunken by the approaching dawn like a beached jellyfish.

But it didn't die. Instead it scraped itself off, calmed itself down and regained its structure.

Or regained *a* structure, maybe looking a little smaller now to Nez. It not only had less mass, but a greater density, like it had learned from flying too close to the sun, underestimating the little girl and her pop guns.

After a minute of the monster pacing, giving the mouth of the wrecked van a wide berth, it wasn't exhibiting so much as a limp and Nez was beginning to get the feeling like they'd missed the only brief window of opportunity they'd had, one that Vicky had died to give them.

"What do we…" Kate started to repeat, the words becoming a mantra.

"I don't know," Nez said, cutting her off, and then glanced over to her, not wanting to look at the arm. As far away and obscured as it was, Nez still got the impression that he could see the tattoos going hazy as the corrosive processes of the monster's digestion began. He was melting Vicky down, taking all that originality she had tried so hard to brand onto herself and reducing it to blood, ink and bone.

Kate did not look as strong as she'd been a few minutes ago when she'd taken control, jostling him out of the way and locking doors. Either she needed a dose or this was what losing hope looked like, what he must have had on his own face, creeping up his forehead into his buzz cut, his scalp humming and his face feeling flushed.

The creature seemed to have an answer to her question, though, as it approached Ken's makeshift burial mound, not limping, but without the fluidity that it'd possessed before Vicky had sand-blasted it with crystal meth.

Kate made a sound, possibly the start of a new question or the same old one that got caught in the back of her throat, but all Nez really heard was "wug" before the words died.

*What is it doing?* If that wasn't her question, it was certainly his.

The creature reached out two tentacles and sunk them into the ground. Four, depending on how you counted them up, as the stalks of each were forked on the ends like little hands.

It struck Nez that these were conservative appendages, not the bone and goo whip the creature had used before, not the powerful grasshopper legs that had sent it over the building. The monster had either lost its flair for grandiosity, or it was being extra careful with Ken, in case the junkie was still toxic, dead and dusty as he was.

Close as the body was to the building, Nez had to go to his toes to watch over the ledge of the window. Shorter than him, Kate wouldn't be able to see much, which was maybe for the better. Whatever the creature was doing with her dead partner, she didn't need to see it.

The feelers extended and then pinched down around each of the corpse's sneakers, squeezing the rubber of the toes and waiting a second before digging down further to the heels. Once it had a firm hold of both shoes, the creature shifted its form, weighing itself down, moving its bones even closer to the ground and lowering its center of gravity. At the top of the mass, Vicky's still-fleshy arm was just another piece of detritus to be floated around, a toothpick to be worked on either side of its nonexistent mouth.

Then the tentacles pulled up and back, not bothering with removing the weight of dirt pressing down on Ken's body, instead yanking at his sneakers, cracks appearing in the semi-packed dirt clod like the fault-lines at the foundation of a doomed sand castle.

There was so little movement, so much conservation of energy going on, that Nez barely had time to register what was going to happen next, that the creature was not only more intelligent than they initially thought, but carried within it the capacity for spite.

The creature puffed itself up, readjusted its grip to include not only Ken's shoes but his ankles, and then tossed Ken's body at the window.

# Chapter Thirty-Three

It wasn't a blowout, but it wasn't a wheezing hiss either, the kind of puncture you can spray with some Fix-a-Flat and then keep rolling. He had a flat tire.

The man named Warren Oates would have to pull over and change it, something that would not only be a pain in the ass, but a setback that could cost him his job, cost the southwest one or two major metropolitan areas, and most importantly: his life.

But he could not allow himself to sweat what was out of his control.

There were enough controllable details for a top-tier soldier like himself to worry about, fixate on, he didn't spend time worrying about what-ifs.

Years ago, before any of this fixer shit, before he'd started worrying whether his or not his ride was conspicuous, could be identified by a civvy, before his name was even Warren Oates, he'd driven a 1987 Lincoln Continental, the last year the model was still rear wheel drive.

He got out and walked around back of his anonymous Asian four-door. *Honda or Hyundai? What does the H stand for again?*

He had checked for the spare and jack before driving off the lot. He used small independent rental companies, something that was becoming harder to find these days, and paid cash. These companies would keep a copy of his license and info on file, but they wouldn't be uploading it into any computer systems, not that the real Warren Oates would probably mind.

The rear tire on the passenger's side was low. He wasn't riding on metal, but he couldn't risk heading any further out of the way to go look for the cop. If he wasn't able to switch out the spare on his own, he would need to roll into a service station.

Popping the trunk, he'd almost forgotten about why he had been riding so low in the first place, the piece of cargo that was at least partly responsible for the flat.

The canister was heavy, hellish to move without help. It had straps on the side, like it was meant to be slung over his back, but it was too full for that. They were still useful, though, for tipping the tank onto its side, where he could more easily pick it up and lower it to the dirt of the shoulder.

He didn't risk putting his hazards on. If he was going to be seen he was going to be seen. If someone drove by he just hoped they were a prick who kept going, not some Good Samaritan he would then have to waste and cover up the pleb's body and car.

Nobody was allowed to see, smell or touch the tank but Mr. Oates, even if they'd never be able to tell what it was. It looked ordinary, like the equipment used by guys who fumigated houses or industrial-strength weedkiller. If he were spotted holding it, Warren could have passed for any variety of workman. It had a small hand pump at the top, was made of heavy opaque plastic, straps, and the sound of jostling liquid inside.

And it was heavy.

Warren groaned, felt sweat instantly drip down and coat the area from his shoulder blades to his ass as he lowered the canister to the ground, careful not to drop it. If he broke the tank open now and spilled any of its contents into the ditch, then he might as well deep throat his gun now, save himself the trouble of changing the tire.

The canister touched down, the sound of grinding dirt the extent of the impact, the bottom of the canister sitting flat. There was no chance of it rolling off, Warren engaging in a serio-comic chase down the interstate.

Unfixing the false bottom of the trunk to reveal the spare, jack and iron, Warren was pleased to find that the canvas was removable, probably meant to double as a drop cloth for any maintenance, but just the right size to throw over the tank. He smoothed the dark cloth over the container, making it nearly invisible to any passersby, of whom there had been none, and then set about fixing the flat.

As he turned the lug nuts loose, having to remind himself not to ratchet up the car first and lose all the leverage, he looked up into the night. Above him, as far into the rocky horizon as he could see in any direction, were stars. The moon was there too, but it was not the main attraction, small and high in the sky. No, out here, in God's country, away from the light pollution, the stars were the thing.

It was like a nature special, his knowledge of what was out there coloring his perception, making him see things, dark purple nebulas, real Hubble shit, that he couldn't possibly be seeing with his naked eye.

The fifth nut twirled loose and he brought his eyes back down to earth, focused himself on getting the car up, the tire off, and the new one on.

For all the serenity he'd felt staring up at the sky, how effortlessly he'd affected his inner grease monkey in loosening the bolts, the rest of the operation set him back what had to be at least an hour. After the fifteen-minute mark he didn't keep exact count. Checking his watch was taking up time that could have been spent struggling with the jack.

The man named Warren Oates needed to get on the road and find that fucking thing. He needed to make the canister do whatever it was going to do and quick, before the daylight came and with it, more witnesses.

# Chapter Thirty-Four

When you're a barfly you get to know your bartender.

Better than you know your parents, better than you know your priest, because your bartender has nothing to hide, has seen you at lows that those other people are likely spared from, kept from, and that's what makes him open up to you, and, conversely, what makes you interested in him.

This meant that Kate knew about Benny's wild streak, his initial vision for Rose's Tavern that the softness, his love of the bar's namesake, had kept him from realizing. Benny would have preferred his roadside bar to err more towards a biker clubhouse, a fortress more than a whimsical Irish taproom, picked up out of Dublin and placed into the Nevada desert.

So even though he'd deferred to his wife's aesthetic for much of the design, on the chicken wire he had been unshakeable. Not only were the windows double-meshed, the glass itself was thick and well insulated, to keep the cool air in and the strain off their electric bill. The wire was there not for protection, but because it made the bar look badass, like a fight could break out at any second and the chicken wire was the only thing keeping the action inside.

It had been Benny's fantasy to own a roughneck bar, the dream of a young man who'd seen the Billy Jack films one too many times, *Born Losers* especially, that had saved Kate and Nez's lives, at least for the moment.

That didn't mean Ken's collision with the window wasn't messy.

The corpse flew towards them like a lawn dart, Ken's expanded chest and collapsed head coming first, the missile top heavy, his arms streaming behind him with enough sway to them that the movement looked lifelike, almost ethereal.

If Ken took a hard turn upwards he'd be able to fly straight to heaven, nonstop, but that wasn't his trajectory and his body slammed into the first layer of chicken wire, the thick, well-moored net doing little to slow him down.

Kate couldn't see the glass breaking. If she was able to it would have been the last thing she ever saw. The shards that made it through the second, interior, web of chicken wire would have collided with her eyeballs and blinded her.

Before the glass could reach them, Nez had already put one big hand over her face as he simultaneously pulled back with his arm, grabbing her in a protective headlock. Both of them dropped to the floor, a trust fall with no regional managers on the other end to catch them.

A split-second later, flat on her back, she felt the glass and blood rain down on top of them.

"Are you alright?" Nez asked, peeling his hand away from her face, the blood around his fingers heavy and dead, sticking his flesh to the thin skin under her eyes.

Before she could answer him, he pushed her up, lifting her to where she was no longer lying on him. She hoped he'd beaten the glass to the ground and hadn't embedded any shards into his back by body-slamming down onto them.

At the window, the collision had done Ken's body some good: the violence of the impact had made him look a little more human. His skull was now half in and half out of his chest cavity, his eye line peeking over his scapula, his neck no longer just a fuzzy lump. Ken was a reverse Ouroboros, birthing himself instead of consuming.

The blood and gristle spread across the stretched-out chicken wire, the glass that was still left stained red and reflecting the light of a million stars, forming a kaleidoscope, turning Ken's body into an unholy mosaic.

The corpse had gotten enough speed, caught the wire just right, that Ken's left hand had poked through one of the honeycomb cells of the inner layer, sustaining minimal damage outside of having his thumb broken backwards and only hanging on by skin, but that injury may have been sustained earlier.

Kate had withstood enough indignities in her life to become a cautious realist, an atheist who'd never fully articulated her worldview to herself but always flinched when she heard anyone imply that *every-thing happens for a reason* or *The Lord works in mysterious ways.* If everything in Kate's life had happened for a reason, was orchestrated by any kind of higher power, then that reason was that the world was better off when Kate was fucking miserable.

Ken's outstretched hand, hanging there close enough for her to grab it, pull him inside to safety, was just one more cosmic "fuck you" to add to the pile.

"We've got to make a decision," Nez said, standing. She heard him dust the flecks of glass off his pants and shirt and move farther into the room to where they'd laid the Jansport.

Kate did not reply, just kept looking at Ken's body, the way it floated in front of the window, a gruesome art installation, perfectly still and held in place by the wire, not falling in even though that's what gravity wanted of it. Ken's blood had solidified, too thick to drip much on the barroom floor. He was covered in a light layer of dust, most of the big dirt and sand clods flying off as he was propelled through the window, but the silt that remained giving him the look of a powdered donut, changing the texture of his flesh to make his body look more statuesque.

Then she focused beyond his body, to the movement out-side, the creature coming closer. Its silhouette took up so much of the window that the light of the stars could be seen through it at its thinnest points, and it was only then that Kate began to seriously wonder about its origins. Whether it could have come from those same stars, the first of many, an invasion force, the fact that the group of them had been trying so hard to escape this little corner of a doomed earth another cosmic joke.

Or was its existence something we did to ourselves? Was the goo something that smelled weird at first, in these pre-beta trials, but would end up being delicious drizzled on popcorn, when whatever scientists were working on it got the formula just right?

Whatever its origins, it was coming up to the window, taking hold of Ken's body again, shaking him free from where he had embed-ded himself in the wire. And Nez was right: they did need to make a decision.

Kate stepped back as the creature pulled, tentatively at first, but the corpse was too stuck for that to do much good. The creature tugged again, leaning back from the window, letting a little more of the star and lantern light in from where the van had rolled parallel with the front door of the bar, not blocking them in but closer now than any other vehicle. If only its wheels were touching the ground and it wasn't now shaped like a horseshoe, they'd be able to use it to escape.

She couldn't see what the creature was doing but it must have readjusted its grip, because Ken's body lifted up and over the window-sill, the metal of the chicken wire squeaking, some of the glass that had caught in the wire shifting free and falling onto the hardwood, breaking.

Once the body was up, suspended, it took one swift tug to get the hand unstuck from the wire, popping off Ken's thumb so that it rolled towards them, Kate having to pick up her left foot so the severed digit couldn't touch her.

*Tag, you're it, girl. Wake up and start counting the stash, I'll make us some breakfast.* She looked down at the thumb, simultaneously wanting to hold it to her heart and squish it like a slug blot out its power to make her weak, sad, to let the hurt in.

Kate couldn't remember having cried once since they'd arrived at Rose's Tavern. This was odd, not only because of the stress, because of the death, but because crying was something she did daily. Letting the hurt drip out one tear at a time until her pressure equalized was part of her routine. She was more regular about it than she was brushing her teeth, scrubbing her bridges not a top priority anymore, now that her teeth were rot-proof.

Either the dirt had neutralized the poisonous corona Ken had seemed to carry earlier, or the monster no longer cared about touching him, had suffered so much from Vicky's shotgun blast that it'd gotten used to the taste. It used more than the two tentacles it had before to hoist Ken out, flip him over and toss him into the packed ground of the parking lot. The body landed with a wet sound, something that would have made her flinch earlier, but now the damage was done, it wasn't him anymore.

Without the glass, the stink of the beast wafted through the window towards them, heralding its arrival even before it was clear that the creature intended on coming in with them, would be there in a moment.

She was thankful it was a still night, that the wind wasn't helping to push the reek along, fill the barroom.

Vicky's arm floated up, letting Kate see that there was no skin anymore, just muscles and sinews, then was sent down as the creature approached. The monster pressed a tentacle through the threshold of the window and plucked at one of the polygons of mesh like a guitar string.

Behind her, Nez worked on one of the bar tables, unzipping the backpack, hurrying. As close as it was, as strong and smart and big and rank and evil as it was, Nez was still fighting, still trying to Mac-Gyver their way out of this situation.

"Get back," he said.

She didn't listen, kept looking at the creature as it moved in, the same way an obstinate child might look directly at an eclipse, realizing the danger to her eyesight but young enough not to give a shit if she ever saw again. She just wanted to see something spectacular.

It pushed itself into the mesh, dividing its mass like thick dough on its first few passes through the tines of a mixer. As the spools of gelatinous flesh moved through the wire, preferring the bigger, distended chambers to the smaller, angular ones, they rejoined on the other side, parts turning back into a whole.

Each of its bones came through the mesh too, the smaller ones having no issue, but the larger ones needing to be pushed, the metal bending to accommodate them.

The creature was halfway through this transition, no more than a foot from her, already beginning to gather some stalks on the floor for support, when Nez put one hand on her shoulder and tossed a small, flaming little package with the other, whatever he had been messing with while she was standing awestruck, maybe even suicidal.

The projectile was a bar napkin, the kind that Vicky had been using with such little success to make the Molotov, but the corners wrapped into a little bow. Kate had seen something like it in the gift shops of New Orleans when she was younger: a juju bag, filled with herbs and spices that would keep the bad spirits away.

Of course, Kate knew the kind of herbs and spices that would keep the monster away, and she wished it would work, but knew it probably wouldn't.

# Chapter Thirty-Five

David Nez lit a second pouch using his first match and lobbed it next to the other one, the first already flashing bright and then smoldering, but not burning as much as he'd have liked. The napkins were too thin, went up too quickly and did not offer enough kindling.

The smoke rose up and touched one of the creature's legs, one of the thin roots it was sending down as it transitioned between the outside and the inside of the bar, a kind of slow-motion osmosis (*how does water travel through the cell wall, class?*). The smoke from the first pouch must have been too low in toxins, because it just moved over the monster's flesh, getting no reaction.

The second ball, the one he'd soaked with Wild Turkey 101, the next highest proof liquor he could find on such short notice, did the trick.

White, silky smoke rose from that flame, the accelerant causing it to burn longer and harder than the first dud. The smoke caused the monster's flesh to ripple, the molecules of the ooze unable to occupy the same space as the meth fumes, causing the flesh to billow, going convex around the smoke.

The nearest tentacle began to drip like a melting icicle before the creature reared up, pulling stakes to leave.

The monster retreated, the smoke grenades working so well that for a second it looked like they would backfire, causing the creature to pull up and away so fast that it dislodged a portion of the chicken wire from the windowsill, snapping the metal in a dozen quick pings.

But they were safe. The creature didn't take the opportunity to bound through the window, didn't want to go over the flames, even though it could have been upon them before Nez could light any more.

Nez sighed and—as if to counter—he heard Kate breathe in

deep.

"Don't do that," he said, guiding her away from the smoke, knowing full well that she wasn't inhaling a sigh of relief, that she was getting high. Seeing her do it, suddenly the smoke was like those seedy hotels on the outskirts of town, the pull that he felt taking him away from his desk job, the fact that if he'd been smart he could have cashed in his chips and gone out in a blaze of hedonistic glory months ago, instead of ending up here.

"So what?" she said, a challenge.

Her resignation showed him how stupid his own was, showed him how much better the next five to fifteen minutes of their lives could be if they just tried.

"So we can make it. You see what the smoke did to it," Nez said, walking her behind the bar, not taking no for an answer. He hoped that her tolerance was high enough, the meth was diluted enough, that she didn't just O.D. huffing on a thick cloud.

Behind them, the pull of the wind outside caused the smoke to float out the window in a thin sheet, forming a force field of protection, not following them deeper into the room. Even still, the room smelled like an electrical fire in a sewage treatment plant.

Once the smoke slowed he would need to light more. It wasn't a permanent solution, but it was better than no kind of perimeter. "It doesn't just not like the taste of this shit, it can kill it, it melts," he said to her, something to keep himself moving forward.

"We can't stay here," she said.

"Exactly what I was thinking," Nez said, using the sink behind the bar to wet a cloth, the water pressure sputtering and dying. No more water, there must have been some kind of electric pump either in the back or in the shed. "Here, wrap this around your face."

He handed Kate the rag, and she looked at it for a moment, like she might refuse because it was dirty, blotched with dust and oil, but then must have realized what an insignificant complaint that would be, considering the situation.

"What about you?" Kate asked.

Nez moved over to the taps, remembered his hesitance to drink this morning, then took down the pull for Bud Light and the one for Pabst Blue Ribbon. The Bud looked clearer so he used the keg to wet his own rag and tied it to his face. The beer was cool against his lips and there was an itch in his throat telling him to suck in and take a sip, his brain telling him it would taste like utility rag.

"It's basically water anyway," Nez joked, his voice muffled by the rag, the two of them looking like train robbers.

He fished in his pocket for his key.

"We can make it," he said, not for the first time, pushing her out from behind the bar. He then checked his boots, that they were on straight, his heels and toes where they needed to be to run.

"Can we?"

"You follow me out. Keep running to the truck. We can make it." Nez hadn't felt this optimistic since basic training, since getting his scores back for the written exam, before the world turned difficult. He was flying. They would make it.

Oh fuck.

He was high.

Where did they leave those pool cues?

# Chapter Thirty-Six

The first thing Vicky Quail saw after regaining consciousness was what she thought was a red ambulance light.

The light felt like home, like rescue, like sitting on her father's lap and watching Three Stooges shorts, like pillows of soft gauze and intravenous fluids she wanted to drink right out of the bag, never mind the needle.

But it turned out the orange/red glow was just a combination of her blood splattered on the lantern and the light shining through it, the added strobe effect either a trick of her imagination or the result of a concussion.

She tried to lift herself and couldn't. Then tried to turn her head and found it a task that, while difficult, proved doable. She looked to her right and didn't like what she saw.

Her arm was gone, not severed but pulled out like she might have tortured a Barbie in her youth, the humerus torn from the scapula.

The flap of skin that connected her shoulder to her arm was still there, though, so when she looked down it formed an optical illusion that made her feel whole for a second before she tried to raise her non-existent hand.

She couldn't spot it in the van or on the gravel outside the windshield, so she figured it must have been monster food, a consolation prize for not getting the whole chicken before it had pecked an eye out.

There was no ambulance, no way to get a belt around the stump because there was no stump, no way to even slow the bleeding one handed.

She was as good as dead.

As good as, but *no, not dead yet*, she had to tell herself. It was strange, even being able to recover consciousness was a miracle. After that much trauma she should have bled out peacefully, drooling onto the headrest of the driver's side seat that was now mashed into the ceiling at an angle.

Moving the fingers of her good hand, reaching around to feel the absence of her arm, she felt the tackiness, the thick sputum webbing the knuckles together. The monster hadn't saved her life when it took her arm, but its gunk had prolonged it, tapered the end of the wound off so she was barely breathing, the hole in her shoulder a coagulate drip instead of a cartoon fountain.

As her wits came back she did a one-handed push-up off the felt of the ceiling to seat herself. This slowed-down bleeding wasn't a recent occurrence, she reasoned, otherwise she'd have woken up in two inches of blood, possibly even drowned in her own plasma.

The thing had been all around her when she'd fired the shot that scared it off. She'd been submerged in it and left soaked. But if the rest of her flesh was being digested, the gunk was working slowly. If the saliva the beast left behind was caustic, she didn't feel any pain, only a tingle all over her body like a blush, her remaining blood humming.

It could have been a reawakening of her senses or it could have been a precursor to septic shock, the open air entering her, ready to kill her. She needed to work fast. There were sounds outside the van that weren't the hoots and chants of victory. She hadn't killed the thing, but she'd at least hurt it, sent it in search of easier prey.

Crooked against the driver's side door and the steering column, she took her hand off the floor and searched her back pockets.

Her ammo could now double as pain meds, as pep pills. She didn't know much about drugs, besides the fact that she was too chickenshit, had too much hate for her mother to ever try anything beyond the occasional toke of weed, but she wondered if the bioavailability of the meth when eaten would even make it worth swallowing.

*Don't think*, she told herself as she squeezed open the zip of the bag and took a pinch of the broken crystals out with two fingers, pushing it under her tongue before giving herself a chance to wimp out.

Vicky tried to tell herself that, because it had a similar consistency, the meth would taste like the salt and crumbs at the bottom of a bag of hard pretzels, the best part of the pretzel, but it didn't. Instead it was more like what she imagined battery acid must taste like ultra-bitter Sour Patch Kids from hell, which made her mouth feel even dryer than when she'd slept with it open, tongue cracking.

She bit her own lip to try and stifle a yelp but that only made it worse, gave her a taste of the monster's goo and caused her to gag.

*No, fuck that shit, don't you puke. Keep it all down and get going.*

She grabbed a hold of the shotgun, held in place against the upside-down dashboard with a coat of slime.

It was time to hunt.

Demolished as the van was, there was still a small triangle of space between the seats and the body of the van. It would have been a tight fit if she had both her arms, but it was easy to wiggle through now that she was slimmer.

Her ass in the front, her torso in the portion of the back that wasn't crushed, she dug through the wreckage for shells.

To arm them, she poured a marble of meth into her mouth after finding each one and spit it into the hull as she went. She did not possess the dexterity that she had when first preparing the dosed shells. Either that or her judgment was somehow impaired, she didn't know what from, the drugs or the trauma.

After she had hocked a loogie into six shells, she stopped looking. It was doubtful she would get one shot off, never mind be able to break the shotgun open and reload two separate times. Before anything else, she broke the gun, filled the chamber and put the rest of the ammo into her front left pocket.

Wiggling out of the back section of the van was harder than getting in.

She was a hopped-up Pooh in the honey tree, her lust for gunpowder and ball bearings sated, but now stuck.

Using her left arm she pushed her body back, touching one of the seats with her ruined shoulder and sending an electric snake of pain through her body.

If thy drugs were quick, they weren't quick enough.

Where was all this euphoria she'd heard about? It couldn't hurt to sniff a little at this point, dead as she was and not worried about an accidental overdose, so she did.

And then gave one more big push, stippling her bare forearm with glass, to dislodge herself from between the seats.

It was only once she was free and into the cab that she realized she would have to army-man crawl over a few feet of shattered windshield and gravel before she was out from under the half-open hood and able to stand up.

She hoped she'd live long enough to do some more damage, but as slow as things seemed to be going with one hand, it didn't look likely.

# Chapter Thirty-Seven

Kate watched the wave crest over Nez as they burst out the front door, the mass of it not behaving like any liquid or solid should act, and she didn't feel awe or fear.

She felt better.

The hurt was gone, even if it would only stay that way for a half hour, before the second stage of the high would kick in and she'd start getting over-analytical taking stock of the minutia around her, buffing a hubcap until it was sparkling, arranging the flowers of prairie weeds into a bouquet before pruning off all the petals, trying to make the things around her perfect.

This was the terror and the wonder of her life, that she could not care less about the bone and blob monster standing at the periphery of their torches.

She gripped her pool cue, holding it high and away from herself, a ball of burning plastic, meth and cash keeping everything in place. Nez had used maybe two thirds of the remaining product to line the duct tape, and then layered in crumpled bills to keep the fire burning longer than the napkins had.

There was no time to test the torches, so they were unsure how long their only line of defense would last. Or that the smoke given off would even be enough to keep the creature from lashing out, ripping their arms off the way it had done to poor Vicky.

It was working, they were a few yards out the door as the creature circled them, its "body language" a cross between a tsunami and a wolf, a wave of mutilation with Vicky's disembodied arm nearly completely assimilated by now, the tiny bones of the girl's fingers floating free.

Why hadn't they thought of this earlier? They could have all three been walking out the front door, buzzed and safe. As the two of them pressed forward, slowly and steadily, Nez making circles around them so there was an invisible ring of smoke on all sides, Kate's mind was a buzz of what-ifs and whys stretching all the way back into her past, stopping at the words *crib death*.

"Hey you guys," Vicky's voice rang out, interrupting Kate's train of thought. Kate told herself that it was an auditory hallucination, but then Nez flung his torch towards the sound as her voice continued. That the small strawberry-haired girl crawling from the wreckage was a visual hallucination would have been Kate's next guess if Nez wasn't running over to her, furiously waving his torch in front of and behind himself, leaving a line of smoke as he did so.

The creature followed him, leaving Kate alone at the border of the parking lot and the path leading to the front door of Rose's Tavern.

What had Nez's exact words been? *Don't stop?* No, that hadn't been it. *Keep running to the truck.*

He'd sure broken that rule quickly, catching sight of the wounded Vicky. He helped her stand, looking unsure where to grip her. The creature moved in and blocked most of Kate's view of the action, but it was translucent enough that she could make out the general shape of Nez and Vicky by his torch.

Vicky was using something to stand, a thin piece of metal propped under her remaining hand like a cane.

"Get down, bitch!" Vicky yelled, something akin to joy in her voice, and it took a hazy junkie moment for Kate to put together what she was saying with what it was the girl was hoisting up.

The shotgun rang out, the muzzle becoming a tube of flame as Kate dove to the ground, stray shot peppering the dirt around her but the sting of a bullet never coming.

◆

They should have traded duties. Vicky could have held half a pool cue aloft a lot easier than she could fire a twelve gauge, weak and with one hand.

But she was under a bit of a time crunch. Nez had peeled his shirt off and stuffed it into her arm-hole, applying pressure as he held her up. She didn't try to stop him, but she got the feeling he was only making matters worse, causing her wound to leak.

She pointed the end of the gun up and screamed out, straining her wrist, only realizing at the last second that she could end up killing the junkette in the crossfire, not exactly the Hollywood ending she wanted for her dad.

Her arm rocketed back, but she held on, her fingers and shoulder throbbing.

The creature split, the effect looking like the same reverse photography trick that Charlpton Heston had parted the Red Sea with. Not her dad's favorite Chuck role, but she wasn't sure how she could incorporate a *Planet of the Apes* analogy into this mess.

She could have said something about the creature's paws, but she didn't have enough energy and they needed to move. The blast had hurt it, but it didn't writhe around and retreat like she'd hoped. Instead the creature kept a cautious pace with them as they limped back to where Kate lay.

The older woman was on her stomach, making small circles in the air above her with her torch, the fire more embers than anything else, but the smoke output still good.

"Get up, let's go," Nez said to her, speaking so fast that his words were a mush. "Everyone into the truck!" he yelled, the exclamation not matching the speed or tone of the previous statement at all, his voice manic.

That's when Vicky realized that they were all high as fuck.

♦

Nez didn't like it, but he wasn't going to argue. He could try tossing Vicky into the cab, but he didn't think that would work. Maybe he had needed her riding in the truck bed.

"I'll come with you, to reload," Kate said, her torch nearly extinguished and hot lumps of melted duct tape flying off as she waved a cloud over the length of the bumper. Embers floated to her shirt and died, and knowing that each was a rapidly disintegrating piece of a twenty-dollar bill made the sight even more poetic. They had gone so far to survive that money was meaningless.

"Fine, help her get up," Nez said, crossing to the front of the truck, unlocking the driver's side door, unsure how to keep the cloud going to stop the beast from jumping onto the hood and destroying the engine block.

While Kate used one hand to fan and the other to boost Vicky into the bed, Nez unslung the backpack and tucked the straps under his windshield wiper blades. The canvas material didn't light easily, but once it did, it looked like it was going to burn for a good long time.

He gave one last wave of his torch before opening the door and hopping inside, the creature keeping its distance now, either suspicious or planning its next move.

He couldn't keep his torch in the cab with him. Beside the risk of fire, there was also the fact that the bandanna pressed against his face was drying out, that he could taste the acrid tang of the smoke on the back of his tongue, dripping down his throat from his sinuses. He didn't know how much meth he could inhale and still stay conscious to drive them out of here.

Reeling back he tossed his torch at the monster, the smoke and ash causing it to take a few steps back, a window of opportunity Nez used to jump in the cab, get things ready.

Inside, Nez adjusted the rearview to watch Vicky finally get a handle on the edge of the truck and lift herself in without slipping.

Aside from her embryonic sheen and the pale, sickly tone it gave her skin, her limbs were shaky. She was either dying of blood loss or going into shock. Nez wanted to write her off, let the grieving process continue for her, like they'd never found her alive, crawling out of the wreckage, but some stupid part of his brain still held out hope, thought that she was tough enough to take the ride, the fight, make it however many dozen miles to the nearest doctor.

It was the first time in a long time David Nez wasn't thinking like a cop, consciously or unconsciously, by instinct or insight, and the freedom that came with that realization made him smile.

# Chapter Thirty-Eight

At first, the wind felt good on Vicky's slime-covered skin. It made her forget about the gaping wound on the right side of her body.

In the beginning of the ride, after she'd gotten used to being anchored, she let Kate wrap an arm around her stomach while she looped the other one through the back window, grabbing onto the passenger's side headrest. It didn't look like the creature was going to pursue them at all.

All it was doing was giving them a head-start, though, turning its mass to watch them move out the driveway. Nez didn't open the truck up like he could've, Vicky assumed he was too scared of dumping the girls out the bed while maneuvering around the big splinters and downed poles.

Behind them, before visibility reduced to nothing in the darkness, Vicky saw the shape of the creature begin to change, a shifting of the flesh and bones. If her time observing wildlife had taught her anything, the creature behind them was raising its hackles.

Instead of knowing when it was bested, in danger, it was giving them nature's universal sign for "I'm going to fuck your shit up".

"Punch it," Vicky yelled, but if Nez heard her, it did not result in a sudden speed increase. Getting nothing from him, Vicky turned her attention elsewhere. "Kate?" she asked.

"Yes?" the junkie replied, the smoldering torch jostling around in the bed with them, a small trail of smoke still streaming behind the truck looking like one of the more vanilla the defenses of the Batmobile. They let it smolder. Getting burned was the least of their worries.

"I need you to go in my front pocket and take out the shells," Vicky said, an unwanted shake in her voice while she was trying to give Kate instructions.

After a bit of unnecessary probing that felt to Vicky like Kate was enjoying the texture of her jeans on her stoned palms, she could feel the bulk of the brass primers ease off her thighs.

Vicky broke the shotgun, exposing the ejector.

"Take out the left one and replace it, please."

Kate did and then reapplied her grip to Vicky's midsection.

Vicky was struck by two uncharacteristically sweet thoughts: that the woman was a fast learner, and that it felt good to be held again, even if she was no David Nez, even if Kate's grip was squeezing the life out of her.

♦

Kate heard the creature before she saw it, bounding out of the darkness on the road behind them.

Best she could tell, Nez had the truck headed north, towards Vegas. Kate tried to strain to think of the geography, put her thoughts in order, whether going north would be the quickest way to find help. But she couldn't think, not with the wet, heavy footfalls behind them, sounding like a Clydesdale trying to reach full stride in mud. Not with her brain working like it was, filled with the clouds euphoria and confusion and speed.

"We need to be further down," Vicky said, her arm shaking as she raised the gun over the lip of the truck bed, resting her hand on the bump of the wheel well. "Let go of it."

Kate did—letting go of the window, not of Vicky—and using her ass muscles to scoot them both down closer to the edge of the bed. The further they got away from the center of the truck, the more tenuous the grip of gravity felt on Kate's body. Every ripple under them seemed fiercer, ready to dislodge them from the truck bed.

A sheet of smoke was falling over the cab, it was not an engine fire but a fire on top of the hood. Kate looked back to see the Jansport ablaze through the windshield, Nez's head cocked to the side to see the road beyond the flames. The bag burned low, the flames too persistent to be extinguished by the wind.

There was an explosion while her attention was turned away and Vicky's left elbow flew back into her gut, Kate's body becoming a backstop for the shotgun's stock.

"Nothing," Vicky muttered, leaning even further forward.

As if on cue it seemed to be the creature's turn to retaliate. The thin wave of smoke rolling over the truck was too diffuse at this speed, the chemical not much of a deterrent, even with the backpack fire still blazing.

For the last few hours, when it had them trapped in Rose's, it had been sluggish, moving with purpose, but now it was a sports car again, its bones arranged in a similar configuration to when it had leapt up and killed Ken.

Kate felt herself yelling, no words, just screaming, as the creature dropped low, its legs seeming to move faster than its body until they halted and it launched itself up into the air.

Nez either saw the creature jump in one of the mirrors or could read the terror in Kate's voice, because the truck accelerated under them, throwing off the creature's aim.

Kate and Vicky were jostled, but it was worth it as the monster's powerful front legs, both bowed like gorilla arms, missed the bumper by inches, slamming back down onto the pavement.

Vicky took the opportunity to fire again over the hatch of the bed and this time Kate saw what was about to happen and tensed her stomach muscles against the recoil.

"Fuck you," Vicky said, in a tone that sounded like she'd made a direct hit, and was happy about it. Kate couldn't see for herself what kind of damage they'd done over the edge of the cab, she was too busy trying to grab onto nothing and keep them both inside.

"I need a re-rack," Vicky said and Kate removed her arm from around the girl. They were both chilly from the night wind, but it was hard to tell if that was less or more comfortable for Vicky.

Did recent amputees get fevers? Did you fight a fever with cold or hot? Evaporation was a cooling process and Vicky was covered in cool alien goo, did that make it better or worse?

It was a bad time to get fixated, stuck in a meth-fueled question circuit. Kate had her hand in her pocket, trying to dig out the shells while Vicky passed the gun backwards, broken and ready to load.

The truck bucked against its suspension, what could have only been a medium-sized pot hole having catastrophic consequences at this speed, with the girls in this position.

Kate felt three inches of wind form beneath her ass, her lower back and the truck bed, then everything slammed back down to meet the unforgiving metal.

Embers and dust flew up around them, some life left in the torch yet, Kate guessed.

Vicky was fine, took the blow to her good side, but the shotgun took an unlucky bounce, hit the opposite wheel well and tumbled over the side of the truck, clattering to pieces along the asphalt.

"You've got to be kidding me," Vicky said, her words beginning to slur, the look on her face panicked, resigned and weak with nausea.

"I'm so sorry," Kate said, her gaze shifting up to look at their pursuer, miles of dead highway and lonesome desert stretched both ahead and behind them, no one around to help.

# Chapter Thirty-Nine

Vicky was cold and pissed off, but mostly cold.

It was a chill deeper than the fact that she was only wearing a tank-top, deeper than the wind howling in and out of the edges of her wound, working at the edges of Nez's shirt. It was the kind of cold that preceded dying.

She wanted to tell herself that she'd gone further than anyone had any right to, avoided certain death more times today than anyone could have. But there was the slapping of giant feet in the darkness behind them, the creature pounding pavement right at the outskirts of the truck's taillights, its body red in the glow. Its presence bothered her, signifying unfinished business.

Usually, it was her tracking wounded animals late into the night, not the other way around, but the same principles still applied, the disappointment and frustration of an unfinished hunt.

"I'm so sorry," Kate said, like the gun was Vicky's favorite toy and Kate had lost it, not that it was their only defense, and Kate too would be dying without it.

Vicky paused, focused on breathing, on steadying hands that were past the point of being steady.

"New plan," Vicky said, feeling like she had to yell, even though the pursuit wasn't that loud, just an engine and a low whistle and some footsteps.

It was awkward, turning over onto her belly to face Kate, but there were certain conversations that couldn't be held back-to-face. Kate was going to have to be a big girl now, was going to have to make amends in maybe the most spectacular way possible, something Vicky was sure no Twelve Stepper had ever done.

Junkies always had things to atone for, Vicky thought, knowing that she hadn't gotten acquainted with Kate and Ken's story, but seeing her mother's face when she looked back at the woman, Kate's fake teeth too straight and bright for her haggard face.

"I need you to do something dangerous," Vicky said. "But we need you now, to make this right." It was bald-faced manipulation, but manipulation for the greater good.

There was a new sound and they were thrown to the side, the embers of the torch touching Vicky's hand, oddly feeling nice and warm while they were burning her, not painful at all.

The creature had jumped forward again, outpacing the truck and ramming the passenger's side with its bulk. Nez took the offensive, pulling the wheel towards the creature and staggering it as they gained speed, the side of the truck too fast a target for the creature to get a grip on. The monster fell back and they had another window of opportunity to talk.

"It's not going to stop," Vicky continued, readjusting herself, her hand on Kate's thigh, the other woman with both hands on her waist. Their embrace would have been intimate under any other circumstances, but now it was merely the best way for Vicky to make herself heard and understood.

"I know," Kate said, interrupting before Vicky got to the hook, the real meat of what she was saying.

"We need that bag," Vicky said, pointing above both of them, the bag smoldering as the wind pelted it, pushed the flames so low they were invisible. "And you need to be the one to get it."

Kate didn't look scared, didn't look too doped-up, she just fixed her expression and nodded.

The older woman stood first, helping Vicky up.

"Keep it steady," she yelled into the back window at Nez, winded by all the talking, not elaborating any further.

Vicky motioned and up Kate went, the sounds of the monster louder again behind them. How many tries until a direct hit, until it was on the bed with them, absorbing them? The third would probably do it.

No, no. Think of something else.

*Car surfing.*

In an attempt to clear her mind, find balance, Vicky tried to think of a film where the stunt was featured, but all her mind kept coming back to was *Teen Wolf*, which was not exactly the kind of classic cinema her dad would have loved and obsessed over.

That she couldn't come up with a good example was fine: people made their own movies, every day. Was that from something too?

Vicky turned her body, getting her left arm as far as she could over the roof of the truck, her grip doing very little to stabilize Kate, her hand on her calf more of an "it's the thought that counts" gesture.

She watched through the windshield as Kate climbed up and stretched her arms down to the hood, trying to find a spot to grab the bag that wouldn't burn her, eventually digging her hand down to the middle of the bag and yanking. The straps were caught up in the wiper blades and Vicky felt her stomach tighten.

This was probably a moment of truth for the junkie, a lifelong reckoning that would somehow exonerate her for all her past mistakes, up to and including dropping the shotgun just a moment ago.

Vicky liked that, that Kate would be getting a nice arc, even if the monster slammed down on the car and killed them in the next thirty seconds. In fact, Vicky didn't just like Kate's perfectly shaped closure, she was jealous of it.

"Got it," Kate yelled, her ass rising into the night air, the woman trying to caterpillar crawl backwards over the roof, Vicky pulling but not doing much to help.

The creature was parallel with them now, something going on inside it, bones being sucked up from where they weren't needed and reconfigured. It was going to try a new tack and Vicky thought she knew what it was.

"Give," Vicky said, not waiting for the woman to sit back down in the bed before pulling at one of the straps, gathering the bag in her arm. She pressed the Jansport to her breasts, tiny flames licking her tank top, drying out the wet mess of Nez's shirt.

And like that, the creature lashed out with its new appendage, no longer jumping but trying to keep pace.

Vicky let herself be taken up in its arm, using her wounded shoulder to scoot Kate back down, away. The woman had done her job, had played a hero's role, but now it was Vicky's turn to show off, to outshine them all, to burn the brightest and the loudest, like she always had to.

♦

Nez watched, knowing that keeping the truck on the road,

moving forward as fast as possible, was important, but still feeling powerless to help, feeling like his part in all this was immaterial.

Crawling onto the roof had seemed a little desperate to him, a little grandiose, so he guessed that it had not been Kate's plan but Vicky's. Kate didn't look at him as she struggled on top of the windshield, single-minded in her pursuit for the bag.

He watched the creature approach in the left mirror, but there was no need to warn them, they probably heard it, and there wasn't much to be done about it anyway.

Their chase may not have started at high speeds, Nez unsure how stable the women would be in the back, but he was certainly pushing it now, hadn't slowed down for the pothole that had sent the gun over the side, even though he wanted to.

He was fighting his instincts now, trying to out-think, not out-feel, the situation. It was a new angle, a new mindset for Nez, and up until now it had kept them all alive.

As he watched the creature's new arm extend over the cab, he couldn't help it, instinct took hold again. The impulse that had lost Nez his job, caused him to discharge his weapon when he shouldn't have and fucked up a good chunk of his life, caused him to step down on the brake.

The creature kept running, as expected.

Unexpectedly, it wasn't alone. Vicky's pale skin and synthetic red hair flashed in the headlights, the creature moving slightly to encompass the center of the road, straddling the double-yellow line, walking to a stop.

With the creature's flesh entangling her legs and midriff, she looked like a mermaid for a moment, an angry ship's mast, flailing, swearing and spitting down at the deck. Then Vicky swung her arm and Nez saw what she was doing, caught a glimpse of the black Jansport as it flared in the night, a moment of stillness allowing its blue-orange flame to reignite.

In the headlights, the truck stopped to watch, he could see that Vicky had rage in her eyes, a madness that bordered on ecstasy.

She threw the bag downward and the creature exploded as the puff of smoke and embers hit it, sinking downward, melting it in two parts that then split again and again.

The creature tossed Vicky, a half of her in each direction, her death assured, hopefully instantaneous. The death was also so over-the-top that it was in keeping with her character, what he'd grown to know and love about her over the last day.

Behind him, through the open back window, he could hear Kate gasp, the beginning of what could be cheers or sobs.

In front of him, he watched the quivering mass of the creature, mostly in two parts, looking like it was trying to hold itself together and failing, smaller pieces of it littering the road and shoulder in front of the truck, twitching. Between these two main parts was the bag, smoldering like a comet without a crater.

Nez revved the engine once and sped towards the parts of the creature, dividing them further with his front and back wheels, the biggest still-moving mass of the creature bouncing off the grill, splattering enough that he had to engage the wipers in order to see the road.

He continued driving, not stopping to recover Vicky's body.

If Nez and Kate died now, killed by a creature that itself looked unbelievably dead, it would have been an insult to the girl's memory.

They drove in silence, with Kate still holding on through the window. The sound she was making was indistinguishable. She could have been crying or laughing.

# Epilogue

The man parked, then swore, then walked around the back of his vehicle and opened the trunk.

Felix heard him swear the same way you might hear a thunderclap bounce around a mountainous region. The voice was everywhere and nowhere, echoing, loud then soft.

Felix was…

Diffuse.

Paradoxically bigger and smaller than he'd ever felt.

The man named Warren Oates struggled to take the tank out of his trunk.

"Hit by a car," he said to himself and the road. "All this time you're running around only to get hit by a car."

He stood beside the canister and gave the lever a few pumps to prime it. Then he snaked a hose from the bottom of the tank and pointed it at a small mass near his foot. It glistened in the morning sun, a glimmer that may have just been a trick of the light, not movement.

Warren sprayed, not wanting to find out.

The pain was indescribable. The connection that Felix had expended so much energy to keep, the blood and bones of the girl too tainted to eat to get his strength back, was being severed, one spray at a time.

The man continued, clearing the immediate area around his

vehicle, killing Felix by ounces.

◆

"Fuck," Warren said, approaching the remains of the backpack, sifting through it with the end of the sprayer, and then looking back to the tire marks.

He walked back to his car, the tank now light enough to hold on his shoulders, but too heavy to be comfortable, he put it down next to the tire. The spare that had taken him so long to fix that the target had moved on from Rose's Tavern, leaving a mess in its wake.

Reaching for the radio, he dialed his favorite dispatcher.

"Hey, darling. It's two-two again. I think I've got a lead on your suspects. From the looks of it they're driving a truck. One or more of them may be injured, so I need you to check the Vegas hospitals."

He waited for a reply. Listened to the dispatcher he'd been talking with all night.

"And I agree, but this is you and me now who have the best chance of catching up with them and we need to work quickly."

Bending to hang the handset up on the dash, the first sensation was like a mosquito bite, getting him through his pants and munching on his knee.

Then there was another, harder, and the man named Warren Oates realized what was happening. It clamped down on his foot, snaking through the top of his shoe, under the tongue, biting with tiny, sharp teeth.

Not wanting to waste a second, knowing the pistol strapped under his jacket would do no good, Warren dove for the canister.

He didn't make it, though, and was plastered to the ground. The little bastards were already making big enough holes to start digging inside of him, moving up his legs like deep vein thrombosis without the added consolation of getting a vacation first.

Looking under the car, down the road, beyond the canister that was so tantalizingly close, he saw them wriggle towards him, all the little parts, some of them finding each other in the morning light and rejoining.

The man named Warren Oates came up with the idea to shoot himself too late, after the things had already torn his off holster, and taken his trigger fingers.

♦

Small and slow as Felix was, it was getting to be dark again before he'd limped far enough north to see lights in the distance.

They were the brightest lights the desert had ever seen and they signaled an improbable oasis, a place for all things to flourish.

# Author's Afterword

I sometimes forget what my books are about.

Not literally. I can recall what happens in my books, the character's names, even what VinnyLovesGorePorn69 wrote about them on his Goodreads (he didn't like the ending to *Mercy House*, go figure).

No, what I mean to say is that I go to a lot of conventions in an attempt to sell my stuff. I lay all my books out on a table, usually have one or two author buddies along for the ride (shout out to my homies Scott Cole, Matt Serafini and Pat Lacey), and then talk to people for three days about my books.

This kind of in-person approach to sales is great. I get to have for-real meaningful conversations with fellow horror fans and sometimes those fellow fans pick up a book. But the side-effect of needing to give people succinct, punchy elevator pitches for multiple books is... well, you start to leave stuff out.

Even though *Exponential* is my shortest full novel at 60,000 words, I still leave stuff out when I discuss it. Let's walk through what an attempted con sale looks like, shall we?

A person approaches the table.

"Hey there, what kind of horror do you like?" I ask. That's the general opener, sometimes the person will be wearing a shirt or a costume or have a tattoo that's of something I like and I'll compliment them appropriately.

"All kinds," they'll say.

"Well, I've got a lot of different things on the table." Then I'll get to pointing. "This is the alien invasion of Long Island, NY. This is a folk horror nightmare. This has killer eels."

You get the picture.

If their eye lingers on *Exponential*, I'll tell them: "This is my giant monster road novel."

Which is true. In a sense. But it wasn't until rereading it in anticipation of this new edition that I realized that this book is much more than that, to me.

Since I maintain a certain social circle on Facebook, I read a lot of status updates by writers. It's not that I'm judging people, but every time I read a writer say "My characters have a mind of their own!" or "My *muse* decided to kill off Jimmy today! Jimmy was my favorite!" Every time I read one of those things a part of my brain makes a rude rubbing gesture. Because I'm of the opinion that emotional storytelling is great, leads to true art, but writers above all else should be workmen. Your "muse" or your characters have a mind of their own to the extent that they can completely tank your story? Doesn't seem like you're working from much of an outline or care about structure, buckaroo.

But reading back over *Exponential*, this is the book that proves my precious writer-opinions are full of shit. The characters in *Exponential* may not steer the ship, but they certainly have a say in the direction it takes to its destination.

Vicky, Nez, Kate and Ken? I love these guys! It's weird. If people at cons want me to elaborate on what the novel's about, I'll focus on telling them about the monster. But Felix is one of the least important characters, even though I like his drippy bone golem butt, too.

For me, this is less a road novel, more of a hangout story. It's *Dazed and Confused* with way more melting flesh.

Reading back over the book was like reconnecting with old friends.

Old friends that, by and large, I deliberately murdered for the entertainment of others.

So, whether you've picked this up randomly clicking around Amazon or were sold a copy by my sweaty, rambling self in-person: I hope you enjoyed meeting my friends.

Best Regards,
Adam Cesare
3/15/2017

# Want More Cesare? Read on to get your fix:

## Download a FREE exclusive ebook
## by visiting www.adamcesare.com

*The Blackest Eyes* is a mini collection of two short stories. This ebook is free for everyone who signs up for *Adam Cesare's Mailing List of Terror*.

What are you Waiting for? Go to AdamCesare.com and sign up today!

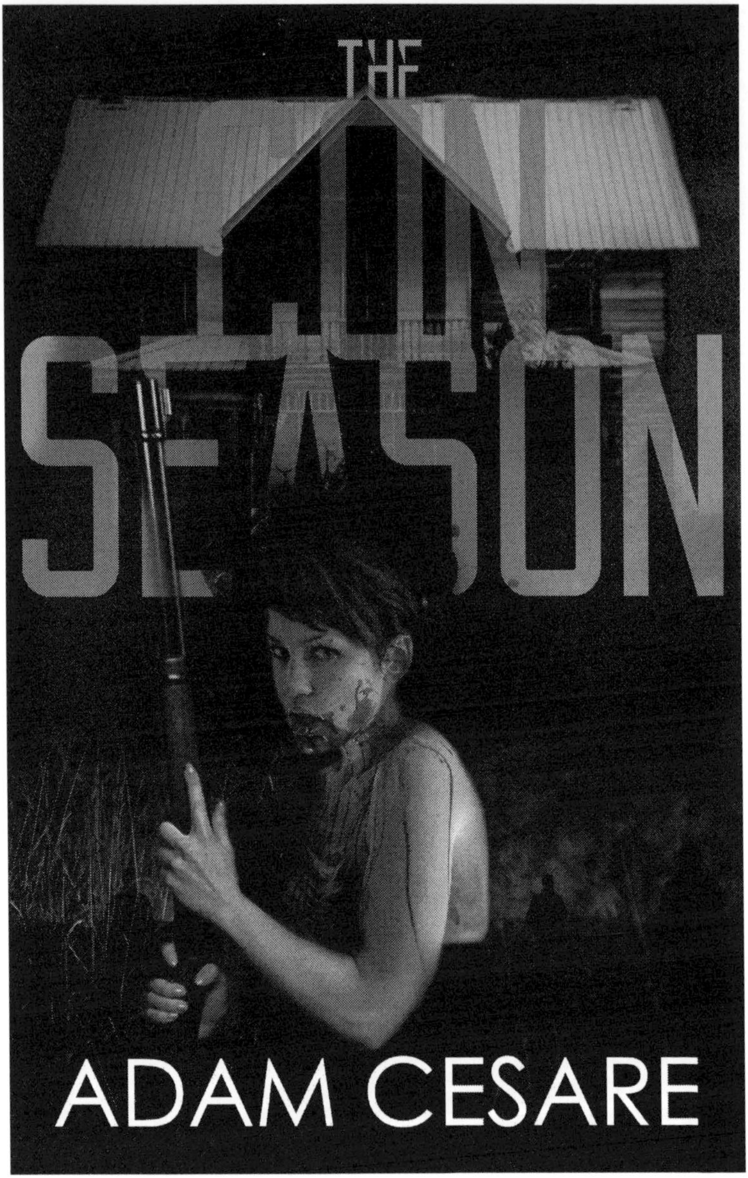
THE
SEASON
ADAM CESARE

THE ITALIAN CANNIBAL HORROR CLASSIC!

WARNING!
BANNED
IN 28
COUNTRIES

ADAM CESARE'S
TRIBESMEN

# VIDEO NIGHT

## ADAM CESARE

# MERCY HOUSE

### ADAM CESARE

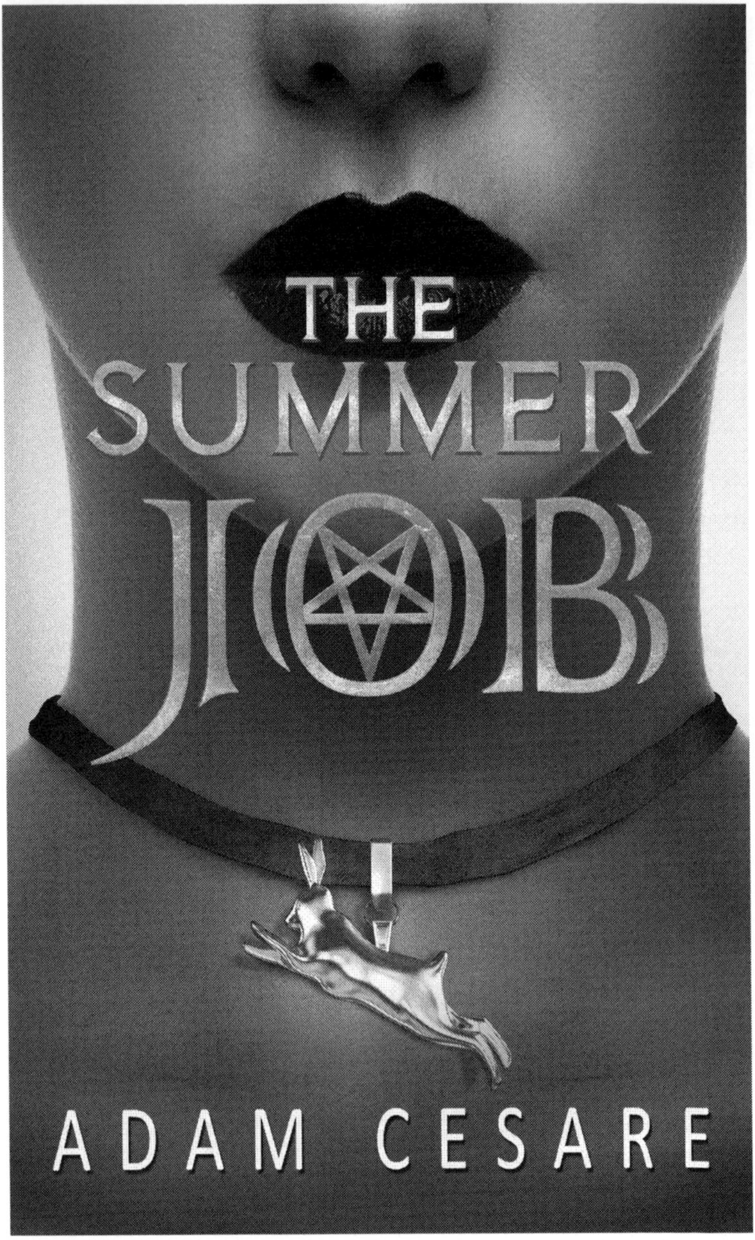
THE SUMMER JOB
ADAM CESARE

# Zero Lives Remaining

"The victims in *Zero Lives Remaining* are different--far from being the typical lost, wide-eyed fodder, these outcasts and obsessives quickly catch on to the truth of their awful situation and come to battle armed in their own strange ways...enough to leave every joystick of the arcade drenched in blood." **–RUE MORGUE**

"While *Video Night* is an exceptional novel,the wistfulness in Cesare's latest, *Zero Lives Remaining*, is twice as thick, the monsters a tad more gooey and intelligent, and the pacing even more insane. The result is a narrative that oozes a bizarre kind of melancholy while celebrating the classic video games and music of a different era while crushing bodies with more speed, creativity, and ease than most current best-selling horror authors put together." **–HORRORTALK**

"Cesare is on the top of his game and delivers possibly hisbest story yet by unleashing a fountain of energy to keep you turning pages and enough horror to make you think twice about touching another arcade game." **–SPLATTERPUNK MAGAZINE**

"I've yet to read an Adam Cesare novel that didn't A) immediately reach up from the page, grab me by the Dennis Rodman lapels, and pull me facefirst into the story, or B) get me to fall head over heels for this world before I'm even a quarter of the way through the book." **–STEPHEN GRAHAM JONES,** *Mongrels* **and** *The Last Final Girl*

**This novella is available in ebook, paperback, and audiobook.**

♦

**For more titles and news about upcoming work be sure to visit AdamCesare.com to sign up for the mailing list or find Adam on Amazon**

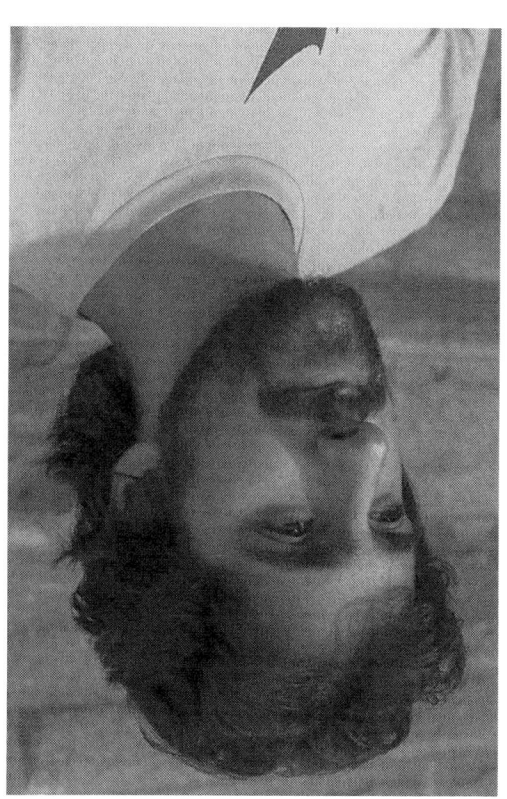

## About the Author

Adam Cesare is a New Yorker who lives in Philadelphia.

His work has been featured in numerous magazines and anthologies. His nonfiction has appeared in *Paracinema*, *The LA Review of Books* and other venues. He also writes a monthly column about the intersection of horror fiction and film for *Cemetery Dance Online*.

His novels and novellas are available in ebook and paperback from Amazon, Barnes & Noble, and all other fine retailers.

Please visit his website adamcesare.com to learn more. Author photo by John Urbancik.

Printed in Great Britain
by Amazon